WHAT OTHERS ARE SAYING...

"Dark, twisty, and mysterious, The Silent Sounds of Chaos kept me teetering on the edge of my seat while frantically tearing through the pages for answers, I was so ensnared within its web."

– Heather Lyons, Author of The Collectors' Society Series

"Wow. Twists, turns, raw emotion, this book literally has it all. I could not put it down."

– Emily Cyr, Author of the Vampire Favors Series

"I was a prisoner from the first word. Watching the story. Living the story. Holding my breath until the very last word, when everything fell into place."

– Kristi Strong, Author of the Kaldalangra Series

THE
SILENT
SOUNDS
OF
CHAOS

a novel by
KRISTINA
CIRCELLI

Copyright © 2016 by Kristina Circelli
Editing by Juli's Elite Editing
Cover by Najla Qamber Designs
Formatting by JT Formatting

http://www.kristinacircelli.com/

Circelli, Kristina
The Silent Sounds of Chaos – 1st ed

Library of Congress Cataloging-in-Publication Data
ISBN-13: 9780976372899 | ISBN-10: 0976372894
First Edition: April 2016

For Kristi
To meeting in weird ways and having it just make sense.

CHAPTER 1

THE BOY HUDDLED in the farthest corner of his tiny closet, bony shoulders pressed up against the cheap, paneled walls of an already falling-apart trailer. In his hands he twisted the thin metal of a paper clip, creating loops and shapes until they formed a stick man, just one of many he'd created to distract himself from the sounds filling his run-down home.

Through the thin walls of his bedroom he could hear the source of his fear—two voices engaged in a verbal sparring match in the next room. One of them he knew, a shockingly thin woman with unwashed blonde hair and sunken blue eyes that, in the past, may have matched his own. The other he knew from many nights such as these, a tall and wide man with frightening pictures on his arms. Their shouts filled him with fear, the woman accusing the man of doing terrible things, the man ordering her to pay or else he'd do those terrible things again.

Their hate, their anger, sent him into the closet, where he often hid when his mother's visitors gave him those strange and calculating looks. His arms wrapped around a soft, yellow blanket almost as big as he was, one he'd kept at his side for as long as his young mind could remember. Face buried in the yellow comfort, he tried hard not to be afraid.

Tonight his fear felt different. *He* felt different, so tired and scared and hurting from a night he'd lived too many times in his young life. But, more than tired—he felt a part of himself fade away into nothingness, only to be replaced by the same hate filling the voices outside his room.

One tiny hand pressed over an ear, the other holding the blanket to his chest, as his body began to rock ever so slightly. He concentrated on the roaring in his ears rather than the thud of a body hitting the hollow floor, or the whimpers from a broken woman who'd given up long ago.

Make it stop.

In his head he whispered the silent plea to anyone who could help him, anyone who could hear the unspoken words of a little boy trapped in his bedroom closet. No one had ever heard him before, but maybe, just maybe, tonight would be different.

Please make it stop.

And then, by magic or miracle, his plea was answered.

I will protect you.

The voice whispered inside his mind, fluttering through his senses in a way that almost tickled. The boy stilled, listening carefully for the voice again, a quiet, high-pitched tone he felt like he should know, but couldn't quite place.

When he heard only the rushing in his ears, he reached out. *Hello?*

I will protect you, the voice said again, a girl's voice.

He knew he should probably be afraid of a stranger magically talking to him, but he liked the sound of this particular stranger. It sounded like music when she spoke, and distracted him from the screeching and thudding going on outside the safety of his mind.

Who are you? he asked, and could almost feel the hesitation on the other end.

I'm not supposed to tell strangers my name ... Are you real?

He huffed. *Of course I'm real.*

How can I hear you?

He thought about it, not coming up with an answer. Nor did he want to admit to silently praying for help, help that came in the form of her innocent proclamation. *Dunno.*

I heard you, she insisted. *I heard you crying in my head.*

I wasn't crying.

Well, if you say so ... Are you sure you're real?

Are you? he countered, trying to comprehend the fluttering in his mind amidst the shouting through the walls.

I think so.

How old are you?

Seven.

Me too. He felt a strange twinge of satisfaction that she wasn't older, and that they had something in common. *Who are you?* Again, he sensed hesitation. *I'm not a stranger.*

Are too.

Fine. He huffed again and squeezed his eyes shut. It was almost fun, blocking out the entire world and focusing only on the person living in his brain. *Then let's pretend to be other people. I wanna be ... an explorer, and have lots of adventures and cause lots of trouble, and run away whenever I feel like it.* He heard her giggle in his mind, and instantly loved the sound. *Who are you?*

I wanna be ... a princess! The prettiest princess in the world who makes friends with everyone and talks to all the animals.

What a girl.

Hey!

He grimaced at himself, forgetting that this strange new girl could hear all his thoughts. *Sorry ... I don't know what to call you. You need a name.*

You think of one, she giggled at him.

He thought, long and hard. *Okay. How about ... I know! Can I call you Snow? Like the princess all the girls at school talk about?*

Can I call you Finn? Like the little boy I saw in a movie at school who ran away to live on the river?

They agreed upon their new names, and, with their introductions, the two children were no longer strangers.

He talked to her through the night, the menacing sounds around him disappearing as he listened to her talk in her youthful, high-pitched voice. She told him about her life living by the beach, with a mother and father who were very nice to her. She liked to read, and watch movies with princesses, and wanted to learn how to swim. It was a happy life, he could tell, and yet, he sensed loneliness in her tone, though he couldn't identify its source.

She listened to him until morning, wondering why he sounded so scared when his words first filtered through her mind, enjoying the way his tone relaxed as the night wore on. He told her about his life in a run-down trailer park, with a mother who paid more attention to strange men and things with weird smells. He liked to skateboard, and hang out with his friends, and hoped to be on a football team someday. It was a hard life, she imagined sadly, and yet, she knew he faced each day with the kind of mischievous-ness only boys could cause.

When she grew quiet, no longer responding, he worried she had grown tired of his stories.

"Don't leave me," he whispered out loud, not wanting her to hear his childish plea. Deep down he hoped she was only tired, that he'd kept her up too late. Her, the voice in his head, a stranger who probably didn't really exist. But he didn't want to give her up, because giving her up would mean accepting the reality around him. And so, instead of saying good-bye or goodnight, the boy now named Finn decided to make her his.

Just before they both drifted off to sleep, one in a closet, and one in a bed an unknown number of miles away, he needed to hear her voice one last time.

Will you be my friend, Snow?

Forever, Finn.

He was in his bed when he woke, though he didn't remember getting there from the closet. The room was warm—air-conditioning was something he only enjoyed at school and the convenience store on the corner—and smelled funny, though that was pretty normal. Flashbacks of the night before played in Finn's head. The shouts. The man with pictures on his arms. The bad things he threatened to do.

"I hate this stupid house and the people in it," he muttered, crawling from the small bed and wincing at the soreness in his body from being crouched in the closet for so long. He stretched as he pulled on a stained white shirt and torn jeans, then walked out of his room, creeping around the corner and hoping his mother was still asleep so he could sneak out of the house. Not entirely sure what day it was, he decided it felt enough like the weekend, and didn't feel like going to school. His favorite hangout was where he needed to be.

All was quiet, which wasn't surprising. Finn didn't bother looking for his mother—or anything to eat—before he slid outside and raced across the front yard. There was a dark car in the driveway; another thing that wasn't surprising, given his mom's frequent visitors. A shout behind him nearly had the boy turning, but he decided against it, picking up his pace until he reached his destination.

The cemetery was his favorite place to go. It was the perfect hiding place, so easy to duck around sprawling oak trees and behind decades-old tombstones. Bad guys covered in ugly pictures couldn't find him here. Plus, he enjoyed the silence found only in the well-groomed gardens. There were no fights, no names being screamed at him. Just him and his thoughts.

This time, though, Finn sought more than the silence.

He sat with his back against the tree he loved most, staring into a patch of yellow flowers, concentrating on his thoughts as he tried to channel the girl who came to him in thought last night. He didn't know what she looked like or even her real name. All he could use was the connection he felt to her, one that hadn't left him since last night. It was like the feeling he got when he sensed someone standing behind him. Except, more welcome, like the person coming to see him was a friend.

Snow?

Only the chirping birds and rustling leaves answered his call. So he tried again. *Snow? Can you hear me?*

Confused by her disappearance, and a little worried she wasn't real after all, Finn plucked a few blades of grass, twisting them in his thin fingers. He refused to believe he'd just made her up because he was scared. Plus, he could *feel* her in his body. Somehow, he knew he wasn't alone, his new friend filling an empty void he'd never even known he had until last night.

Snow? Do you ... do you still want to be friends? The question made him sigh and look down at the grass. He'd worked the blades into the crude shape of a person, with rounded arms and legs and a frayed head.

"Fine," he said to the grass with a smirk, just as his stomach growled. "You'll be Snow since she doesn't want to talk to me anymore."

Torn between disappointment and hunger, Finn chose a brief moment of play, imagining his new friend Snow in her fancy life somewhere else, with parents who loved her. Though, he couldn't imagine not being able to swim. *That's just weird. Who doesn't know how to swim?!*

The grass figure moved atop the ground smoothly, over to a piece of fallen bark. "Make me some bacon," Finn murmured to a nonexistent parent, then danced the character on top of a rock. "And you, put on some car-

7

toons!"

As his mind replayed old cartoons he sometimes watched at friends' houses, Finn let himself drift out of the real world. The cemetery was the only place he could escape and he intended to enjoy every minute of solitude.

"Hey!"

A call behind him had the boy turning, seeing one of the girls who lived down the street from him standing at the metal fence surrounding the cemetery garden. He liked her, especially since she was good at racing and never asked to come inside his trailer. "What?"

"Cops are at your house!"

Finn was on his feet in an instant, shoving the grass woman in his pant pocket before jogging over to the gate. "What do they want?"

"How should I know?" she retorted, dark hair blowing in her face when the breeze picked up. She pushed it back with a grimace. "Ma said to come find you and let you know."

They ran back together, his friend offering a quick wave before turning at the end of the street, leaving Finn to make the rest of the trip alone. When he approached, he saw the same car in the driveway, except now there was a man and woman standing by the back. The woman was writing something on a pad of paper sitting on the trunk while the man—dressed like a cop—stood watch. Both turned when he all but skidded to a stop in front of them.

"Who are you?" Finn challenged the woman before either could speak, breath heavy from the run. He crossed his arms in a childish attempt to look tough, the move mimicking the sneer crossing his face at her nice clothes. People who dressed like that didn't come into his neighborhood unless they wanted something. And when they did, they usually wanted something bad. The fact that she brought a cop along told Finn this woman was trouble.

With a gentle smile, the strange woman lowered herself to her knees so she was at the boy's level. "Hi, sweetie. My name is—"

"I don't care. What do you want?"

Now the policeman stepped forward, his expression just as gentle. Finn was surprised, given how snotty he knew he sounded, and since cops were never nice when they came knocking on doors on his street. "Son, we got a call from one of your neighbors about some loud noises last night. Are you okay?"

"Don't I look okay?" The question wasn't meant to be answered, and he followed it up with another. "When are you leaving?"

The woman continued to stare at him, her bright eyes seeming to see enough to make him uncomfortable. "Are you okay, sweetie?"

His back straightened at that. "I'm fine. Just playing with my friends. I'm going to get some food now."

Finn was surprised when they let him leave, though they didn't drive away like he expected them to. Sparing them a suspicious glare, he stomped up the front step and slipped inside, locking the door behind him.

"The hell you been telling people?"

His mother's palm met his cheek just seconds after he stepped inside. Finn could only hold the side of his face and stare as she raged, fury mixed with fear swimming in her eyes. She spun around and dropped to the floor, rooting through one of the kitchen cabinets. He knew what she was looking for. She only ever paid that much attention to one thing, though he was surprised she actually had to look for it. Glancing around, he saw it was weirdly clean for once, no cans or bottles on the floor or cigarette butts in the ashtray.

He didn't have time to wonder where all the junk had gone or who cleaned up before his mother pulled out a glass bottle and swung back around to face her son. "You think you can get somethin' better out there? Think you *deserve* somethin' better?"

"No," he replied quietly, staring at his feet. "I didn't talk to anyone."

"Then why are those people outside, huh? Why did they want to come in here and talk to me? To you?"

"I don't know." He wasn't lying, which made her anger even more hurtful to the child. "I don't know who they are, I swear."

Bony fingers gripped his chin, jerking his head up so he was forced to look into her eyes. His mother was in one of her raging moods, but she was also scared—and that scared him in return. "Well I know who those people are," she told him, chapped lips pulling back into a snarl. "And let me tell you, boy, if you talk to them, and they get you, then your life will be hell. You hear me?"

His life was already hell, though he didn't voice that opinion. "I hear you, Momma. I promise I didn't talk to them. I remember what you said."

"You better. You better never talk to anyone. People are liars. People will take everything you got until you're on the streets. You want to be on the streets?" she repeated the words he'd heard his entire life.

"No." The reply was but a whisper, though there was an edge to it. An edge she heard, and reared back to smack him again, but he yanked out of her grasp and darted away to the safety of his room, back to his closet with the soft yellow blanket lying forgotten on the floor.

Curling up around it, Finn pulled the grass figure from his pocket and traced his fingers over it, deciding not to call for Snow again. She didn't need to know about the life he wished never existed at all.

CHAPTER 2

T HE GIRL CURLED up in the top corner of her bed, snuggled beneath a soft star-patterned blanket and listening to the sounds of morning time just outside her bedroom door. Her parents' voices echoed through the wooden door, laughing as breakfast was made and plates set on the table for their first Sunday meal.

She knew those voices, loved them with all her young heart. One belonged to the lady who smelled like caramel, with her curly brown hair and friendly eyes that always seemed to be smiling. The other belonged to the man who laughed like Santa Claus, with his thick, dark hair, equally dark eyes, and big hands that made her feel safe each time they picked her up for a hug.

She hadn't known them long, but, already, she'd come to love them.

Sunlight blinked through her curtains, urging the girl to rise. As she did, memories of last night came to mind.

The voice. The boy. The conversation that lasted until she fell asleep. She took a moment to reflect on that conversation, remembering how she'd been lying in bed, staring up at the glowing stars stuck to the ceiling and feeling so alone, when a voice suddenly spoke inside her head.

Please make it stop, the little boy had said.

Perhaps she should have been afraid, but instead, she was intrigued, and a little worried for the boy who sounded so scared as he pleaded for help. Of course, he refused to admit he was afraid, or that he was crying and called for help.

Boys. The girl shook her head to herself and crawled out of bed, making her way down the hallway. She liked talking to him, even if he was a stranger. She didn't have many people to talk to in this new town with new kids who already had friends of their own, and the boy who called for help was all hers.

Her young mind couldn't process the possibilities of his voice in her head, but then, it didn't need to. She had a friend. How she made that friend didn't matter.

"Good morning, honey," the lady at the stove greeted when she walked in the kitchen.

"Good morning," the girl replied around an exaggerated yawn. Her hopeful sapphire eyes that perfectly matched the pale hue of her hair turned up to the frying pan. "Can I have some pancakes, please?"

"Silly goose, you know you don't have to ask." The lady smiled down at her. "You take a seat at the table and we'll serve you up a nice, big breakfast. How does that sound?"

"Good!" The girl did as she was told and took a seat across from the man with the Santa Claus laugh. He scrunched up his face at her, crossing his eyes in a way that made her giggle. She liked it here, with these people. They were funny and nice, and liked it when she laughed.

When the lady set a plate of pancakes and eggs in front of her, the child nearly bounced up and down in excitement. "Thank you, Mrs…"

Her voice trailed off uncertainly, but the lady who tucked her into bed last night wasn't fazed. "Sweetie, you know you can call me Mommy, if you want to."

She did want to, desperately. "Thank you … Mommy."

Her new mommy—the best mommy—leaned over and kissed her forehead. "You are most certainly welcome, my beautiful little girl. Now, dig in. I can hear that belly rumbling all the way over here!"

The girl giggled again and did just that, stuffing her mouth with the best-tasting food she'd ever had. After a few minutes of eating, the man she guessed she could call Daddy spoke up.

"How did you sleep, sweetie? Do you like your room?"

She loved her room. Her beautiful room, with her own bed and her own toys to play with. It was the best room she'd ever seen, and her first night had been the best night of her young life. "I love it," she answered honestly, though she did leave out how scared she had been. Even the nightlight in the corner couldn't cast out all the shadows that worried her seven-year-old mind.

In fact, she'd been fretting over those very shadows, silently praying for them to leave her alone, when she heard the boy's voice in her head asking for help of his own. Talking to him and earning a new friend had helped her get over her fears.

"My friend helped me fall asleep," she put in inno-cently, stabbing at a bite of pancake with her fork.

"Oh? Did Amelia tell you more bedtime stories?"

"No." Snow swallowed and wiped a glob of syrup from her cheek, thinking first about her new big sister who shared her room and was still sleeping upstairs, then her new friend. Amelia was nice and talked to her after they were both tucked in, but she fell asleep fast after that, leav-ing Snow to adjust to her new room alone. "My friend. He said my room sounds nice."

She didn't see the look her parents shared across the table. "Your friend?" her mom repeated. "Who is your friend?"

"His name is Finn."

Her mom laughed, though Snow was too young to hear the relief in the sound. "Finn, huh? Kind of like Huckleberry Finn?"

"I think so. He wants to be an explorer and go all over the world and see new places. He doesn't like his house so he wants to see lots of others and make friends everywhere he goes." Finn had told her all those things during their long talk last night. He had big dreams for a little boy, dreams she admired. She'd never thought that hard about her future before and what she wanted to do when she was a grownup.

Her new mommy tucked back her hair and nodded. "Well, Finn sounds like fun."

"He is. We talked to each other in our heads. He's my age." She told them more about her new friend, as much as she knew, anyway. By the time she was finished her plate was empty. Carefully, she scooted off her chair and brought the plate to the sink. Manners were important to her. She had to clean up after herself to make sure her new parents wanted to keep her. She'd do anything to avoid going back to her old home where there was no one to want and love her.

At the sink, she heard whispers behind her, words like *imaginary* and *worried* and *doctor*. She hoped her new parents weren't mad she was talking to Finn. Even though she had just met him, she didn't want to let him go and didn't want them to think he was bad.

Suddenly concerned, Snow turned from the sink. Her expression was somber as she faced her parents, her father with a smile on his face and her mother looking concerned. "Finn is my friend. He's nice and I like talking to him."

Her mommy smiled and gestured for the child to come over, waiting until the girl climbed onto her lap. "Of course he is, sweetie." She held Snow against her, one hand gently patting her hair. "And I like his name. Is it his real name?"

"No," Snow answered automatically. "I remember what you told me. Since we're strangers we came up with fun code names! I chose Finn for him. I like it. It's fun to say."

"It is fun," her mother agreed, shifting so she could look down at her daughter. "What does he call you?"

"Snow."

Next to her, Snow's father chuckled. "Snow? Does our little girl like to run outside and catch snowflakes on her tongue?"

"No." Snow giggled. "Because I like animals and want to be nice like a princess."

"A princess, huh?" he repeated, one hand lifting to his

forehead dramatically. "Royalty in our family! Honey, did you hear that!" he said to his wife, who raised her eyebrows playfully. "That must make me the king."

"King Daddy," Snow confirmed, picking up a pen and tapping him on both shoulders as she'd seen people do on TV.

"I like the sound of that. And I think Snow is a wonderful name. You just tell this new friend Finn that he better be nice to you or else he'll have to answer to me. And you just remember what we told you about talking to strangers."

"I will."

And so the girl now named Snow tucked it away in her mind that her new friend came with rules, rules she knew better than to break.

Dirt kicked up beneath worn sneakers as Finn pushed off the defensive line, aiming for the quarterback. He was small and quick, his wiry frame making it easy to slip between the other players. Two hands shoved the other boy to the ground before the ball could be thrown. He landed with a grunt and glared up at his opponent.

"Geez, you didn't have to push me," the boy complained, shooting Finn a dirty look. "It's *touch* football. Chill out."

Ignoring him, Finn jogged back to his team, feeling victorious and quite pleased with himself. He'd been amazed the older kids, kids he'd just met in the field in the back of his school, had even invited him to play. Now that he was in the game, he had to be the best. Having seen his friends teased and shoved by other older students in the past, he'd made a promise to show them just how tough he was. Finn wasn't going to let them push him around if he could do the pushing first.

One of his teammates in the game of pickup clapped him on the back. "Awesome block, dude!"

Finn bit back a grin. Now wasn't the time to celebrate and act like a kid, not when the game was on the line. It was important to look tough. No one messed with the tough kids and thought they could run them down on the field.

When they see how much you don't care, ain't a person out there who can hurt you, his mother had once told him. And, for once, she was right. She didn't care who and what she was, and no one in town could bring her down.

He kept that in mind as they got into position again, his concentration focused on the quarterback—a big kid who was at least four inches taller and a good ten pounds heavier. Overhead, the sun beamed down from a cloudless blue sky, warming their backs and lighting the way for more awesome plays. At their feet, ankle-high grass clung to their ankles, leftover morning dew making their runs slippery.

The ball hiked into the opponent's hands. Surging forward, Finn pushed past the center, spun in a circle to avoid a two-hand touch, and reached his destination. His shoulder pounded into the quarterback's chest, bringing them both down. Finn was back on his feet in seconds, breathing heavily yet triumphantly, not even noticing the dirt caked in his hair or the scraped skin on his knees. The other boy tossed the ball to the side before getting up slowly, rubbing at the sore spot on his chest and glaring over at the new kid they'd made the mistake of feeling bad for and letting join the game.

"What's your problem, man? You don't have to be such a jerk."

Finn glared at the boy, who was brushing off his jeans. "Don't get mad at me. Not my fault you're so slow."

"Whatever." Already dismissing his opponent, the quarterback walked away, back to his team, gesturing with a thumb over his shoulder at the "new kid with serious issues."

Finn heard the laughing jabs from his place at the edge of the huddle. He wasn't a jerk, he considered. He was tough. The quarterback clearly didn't understand. Football was not a game where people *chilled out*. It was about winning and being the best. This boy wanted him to play like a girl, to be weak. He refused. Weak people got hurt. Weak people died.

Before he could come back with a retort, Finn was hit with a wave of sadness, one he recognized not as his own, but belonging to the girl he'd talked to only once. As the feel of her presence filled him, he realized Snow was back; he realized how much he had missed her, how complete he now felt knowing she was with him.

But he didn't like the sadness. It was overwhelming, a sensation he didn't know what to do with. It made him feel vulnerable and too much like the kind of person who could be hurt, like his mother said. So instead of being sad, he channeled a different emotion—rage. Yes, anger was easy. It was familiar. Anger he knew what to do with, even if it meant being a jerk and pushing other kids to the ground.

Before he could think to ask Snow why she was sad, he had to get rid of these feelings. They were too much for his small body. His young mind was barely able to process his own emotions, let alone those of another. He stepped forward, about to shout the boy's name and start a fight right there in the middle of the field, when the sadness was replaced by a voice whispering his name.

I wish Finn was here.

The wish stopped Finn in his tracks. He heard her so clearly and felt her need for a friend deep in his heart. Was this what she felt when she heard his plea the night they met? A shout from one of the boys on his team had Finn looking up, but he ignored them, turning around and walking in the other direction to the sound of their questions being called at his back.

They didn't need him. They didn't even like him. Called him a jerk with serious issues. These boys weren't his friends. But Snow was, and she needed him. He was going to be there for her like she was the night he hid in the closet.

Finding a tree far away from everyone else, Finn sat down and leaned against it, closing his eyes. It was easier to concentrate on her voice that way. The more he focused, the less anger he felt, replaced by a deep desire to make his new friend happy again.

He'd know what to say to them, Snow's voice came again.

She didn't seem to know he was listening, or maybe she didn't know he could, he wondered. So he made his presence known by asking, *Say to who?*

CHAPTER 3

ALONE IN HER little corner of the playground, Snow pushed off the ground, swinging lightly beneath the afternoon sun. All around her children played, laughing with one another as they conspired with friends and released the pent-up energy that came from a morning sitting in a classroom. Snow watched them wistfully, wishing she had friends like that, wondering why her own invisible friend had left her so quickly.

It had been one full week since she met Finn, that voice in her head she knew, she *knew*, wasn't imaginary like her parents thought. He'd felt too real inside her mind, like he was walking across her brain and sending her his thoughts by shouting them in her ears. Their conversation had been new and exciting, and made her move to her new home less scary. But believing he was real also made her sad. He'd promised to be her friend, then left her all alone, and her feelings were hurt.

With a sniffle, Snow pushed her long, blonde hair out of her face and stared out at the playground, watching a race in progress. She wasn't a very fast runner and was never invited to compete with the other kids in her class. In fact, she wasn't invited to do anything with the other kids. Amelia had lots of friends and sometimes let her sit with her or join in on conversations, but it wasn't the same as having her own friends to do stuff with. Everyone thought she was a weird girl. Some even told her she was too skinny and that she was too quiet.

"Hey!" a shout to her right had Snow jumping. She looked over to see Davey, a boy from class, standing with a small group of kids. "This is where we play."

Sad, and a little scared, Snow nodded and slid off the swing. She was used to being bossed around by the other students at school, and even the teachers, who were usually grumpy and just wanted to get the day over with. When she made to pass the boy who was clearly in charge, she felt a hand on her arm. "Hey," Davey said again. "What's it like where you're from anyway? You know, at the pet store?"

Snow's blue eyes looked up at the boy, filled with hurt. "W-what?"

"We all know where you really came from," he sneered. "Everyone knows your parents aren't really your parents and they picked you out at the store. So what's the pet store like? Or did they find you in a dumpster?"

Snow pressed her lips together, determined not to cry in front of the kids who were now laughing at her. It wasn't the first time she'd been made fun of because of her parents. Or, rather, because of where she came from. They didn't understand what it was like to have a mom and dad who didn't want her, so why would they understand how it felt to finally have parents who did?

With another sniffle she yanked her arm back and ran. Laughter followed her, making her run faster, away from the mean kids with even meaner words. She found a quiet corner away from the playground and sat with her back against the brick wall, pulling her knees to her chest and lowering her head so no one could see her cry.

I'm not from a dumpster, she thought miserably, remembering the day her new parents came to get her from the group home and how happy she'd been. She'd already known them, having met them several times before and visiting their house. They'd been so nice, so loving. They wanted her, even if her real parents didn't.

I wish Finn was here. He'd know what to say to them.
Say to who?

Snow stiffened at the extra voice in her head, the decidedly boy voice that belonged to just one person. A smile crept across her tear-stained face. *Finn?*

Snow? Where have you been?

Where have you *been?* she returned, annoyed by the question but grateful for his voice. *You stopped talking to me.*

Silence met her thoughts before, *I tried to talk to you but it didn't work. But then I heard you wishing for me.*

Snow frowned, thinking over his response. The first time she'd talked to him, she heard his words whispering across her mind, wishing for someone to make it stop. This time, he'd heard her wish for him to be there. Maybe, she considered, they had to need each other, like invisible superheroes coming to the rescue. She liked the sound of that.

If you say so, she returned, not sure how to continue.

...So, who would I know what to say to?

Brought back to the moment, Snow sniffled again and told him about the mean kids on the playground, about the fact that she was adopted, about the loneliness she sometimes felt because no one seemed to understand. The other kids called her a fake daughter, and liked to make her feel bad because her real parents, whoever they were, didn't want her.

You should have punched him in the nose.

Despite the sadness creeping into her heart, Snow laughed at that, shaking her head. She couldn't imagine herself ever doing something like that. *That's not nice, Finn.*

So? After a hesitation, he continued, *Fine, no punching. But you should at least say something to him so he knows he can't be mean to you.*

Like what?

She listened carefully, eyes widening at the response she never would have thought to say on her own. The comeback was so mean, sure to hurt anyone's feelings. It would certainly hurt hers. When he was finished he ordered her to go say it to Davey. It took some goading, but she finally picked herself up off the ground at Finn's urging and marched back to the playground, spurred on by a sudden burst of courage she guessed came from her friend—though she didn't take the time to marvel at how she could feel what he felt.

Back at the playground, Davey and a four others were standing in a crowd, laughing at something. Or someone. Their laughter stopped when she approached. Davey stepped to the front of the group and crossed his arms.

"What do you want, pet shop?"

Look tough.

Snow squared her shoulders at Finn's command. Then paused, suddenly unsure of what she was about to do.

Say it, Snow. Be brave and say it. Don't be jealous.

Biting back a sigh, Snow said firmly, "Don't be jealous."

Davey frowned and looked around before asking, "Jealous of what, you freak?"

Cross your arms and say it.

She did what she was told. "That my parents picked me because they knew I was the best. Your parents are stuck with you."

The frown turned to a sneer as Davey slid a step closer and went nose to nose with Snow. "And what's that supposed to mean?"

Your parents can't even give you away. No one—

"—would even want a loser and a stupid kid like you," Snow finished, speaking the words at the same time Finn repeated them in her head. "I feel sorry for them. Everyone feels sorry for them. You just don't know it."

For a moment the playground fell silent, everyone watching the two at the center of the commotion, one with his hands curled into fists and the other fighting to keep her knees from shaking. After a tense moment, Davey took a step back and lowered his head, but not before Snow saw the threat of tears in his eyes. The boy stalked away, yelling at his friends to get away from him, and she watched him leave.

Did it work?

Snow nodded. *Yeah. I think he was crying.*

Good. He deserved it.

She wasn't so sure. She didn't like hurting his feelings, even if he'd done the same to her. That wasn't what a princess would do.

Four hours later Snow sat at the kitchen table, both her parents seated across from her. She could tell by the stern looks on their faces that they were angry with her, though she wasn't entirely sure why. She hadn't done anything bad lately. All her clothes were folded and put away, her dishes washed after every meal. Certainly she couldn't have done something wrong already.

"We got a call from the school," her mom said, looking at Snow expectantly. Her stomach dropped as she now knew what this was about. "You said something that wasn't very nice to a little boy, didn't you?" Snow swallowed hard and nodded. She could have lied, but that would be wrong, and she really wanted her new parents to like her. "What did you say?"

Meekly, she repeated the words, her eyes on the table. After she was finished she thought about how cruel they were and wondered why she was so easily convinced to say them. She wanted to blame it on Finn, but deep in her heart knew it was her own choice.

"Why would you say something like that?" her father asked.

"Because he said I came from the pet store or maybe the dumpster." The tears came before she could stop them, this time not afraid to let other people see her cry. Through the burry vision she didn't see the way their faces softened, but she did feel her mom's arms wrap around her as she was pulled into her lap.

"Sweetie, you know that's not true," her mother soothed, one hand stroking her hair. "You are our daughter and we love you no matter what. Never let anyone tell you differently, okay?" When Snow nodded, her mom wiped the tears from her cheeks. "But in this family we have manners, and we don't talk meanly to people no matter how mean they are to us first. Now, who told you to say something like that to Davey? I know my sweet little girl wouldn't do that alone."

Snow fell silent, refusing to get her friend into trouble.

"Did one of your friends at school tell you to say that?" her mom continued, still hugging Snow, who shook her head. "What about Amelia?" Another shake of the little girl's head.

"Did Finn tell you?" her father asked from the other side of the table. Though Snow didn't respond or move, her parents knew the truth by her refusal to confirm or deny. "Well, if he did, it sounds like Finn isn't very nice."

"He is!" she insisted, spinning around to face her father. Her eyes were wide with the fear of her parents not liking her friend. "I was sad and I wished he was with me so I could have a friend. Finn didn't want me to be sad and he wanted to stop all the kids from being mean to me. He just wanted me to be brave."

"Being brave isn't the same as being cruel, honey," her mom put in. "Sometimes being brave means letting go, even when that's the hardest thing to do. There will always be people who say things that aren't nice, but you can't stoop to their level. You have to hold your head high and let things like that go. Otherwise you say bad things back, and then you are just as bad as them. Do you understand?"

She didn't, but chose not to say so. It didn't make sense to let go of people being mean, but, Snow considered, she didn't like how it made her feel to say those things back anyway. It wasn't princess-like.

"Now," her new mommy repositioned Snow on her lap so they were face to face, "no more unkind things. You can't talk to Finn if he's going to tell you to be bad, got it?"

Snow nodded stoically, then hugged her parents when they finally smiled. She didn't want to upset them, because, deep down, she really was afraid they'd return her to the pet store everyone thought she came from. All she ever wanted was a family who loved her, and now that she had one, she'd do anything to keep them.

MOMMY SAYS I can't talk to you if you make me do mean things.

Snow curled up in bed that night, arms wrapped around a stuffed dog as she closed her eyes and imagined Finn in her head. She didn't know what he looked like, so for fun she imagined herself with really short hair and dirty cheeks and boy clothes. The image made her giggle.

His reply came almost instantly. *I don't want to stop talking to you.*

It made her happy to have a friend who wanted to talk to her even if she was so different from him. *Then I can't be mean. I have to be nice to people, even if they say things that hurt my feelings.*

That's stupid.

Snow giggled, but then sobered almost instantly. Even if she agreed she couldn't say so. *It's not stupid. It's nice. I want to be a nice person.*

Fine, no more mean things. She could swear she heard him sigh. *If someone hurts your feelings, just tell me. You can be nice and I'll be mean enough for both of us.*

She didn't know what that meant, but it sounded like a fair enough alternative if it meant she could keep talking to Finn. *Deal.*

CHAPTER 4

FINN SAT ON the front step of his trailer, leg bouncing as he stared out at the patch of brown grass that served as a front yard. He wanted to run all over it. He wanted to dig holes. He kind of wanted to throw up in the broken flower pot next to where he sat.

Sitting on pins and needles, it was all he could do to contain himself to this little stoop beneath the blistering summer sun. He really wanted to go inside and get the basketball he'd left in his room, but knew he had to wait until the noises coming from the living room stopped. To keep himself as busy as possible he'd started carving a piece of bark into the shape of a lady using a rusty pocketknife one of his mom's "friends" had lost in their couch. He wasn't a good artist, but after a while his animated fingers carved something that looked vaguely like a person.

He'd found one of the bottles his mom had hidden in the back shed and downed a good chunk of the clear liquid, curious as to why she was always drinking it. Though he found the taste bitter, he couldn't deny how awesome he felt in this moment. Full of energy, bursting at the seams to go and do something super fun, and yet, kind of like the whole world was swimming in front of his eyes and only a long nap could make it all go back to normal. Concentrating on the fuzzy air made it easier to block out the sounds he'd long ago learned never led to anything good for him.

You feel weird.

Snow's voice popped into his mind. Finn smiled, his bouncing transforming to a kind of side-to-side action on the step. It didn't surprise him that Snow would show up. Over the past few years they'd learned to control it, whatever *it* was, able to call on one another whenever a conversation was desired. They'd even started to feel what the other felt during times of fear, anger, or excitement. The feelings were usually a bit subdued on the other end, but they were strong enough to help them through any situation, knowing their mystery friend was by their side, wherever they were somewhere in the world.

They still didn't know each other's real names, where the other person lived—it was exciting, in a way, kind of like they were superheroes waiting for their chance to save the person who had become their best, mystery friend. Sometimes they ignored the feelings swarming throughout them, other times their thoughts still crept in during times of need, and the pair had come to accept casual comments whispered in their minds here and there.

Finn liked that she was always there. A constant friend, someone who kept him feeling light and happy and never alone.

Can't sit still, he answered, wondering if his voice sounded as jittery as his heart felt. *Got to move. Got to play*.

She was quiet before asking, *Are you full of ... finnergy?*

Finn paused, his bones nearly quaking in the stillness as he thought over her question. Then he burst into giggles, hearing her laughter echoing his own. *Finnergy*! He repeated the word over and over in his mind until they both were gasping for air, Finn nearly falling off the step as he clutched at his sides.

It had been a long, long time since he laughed. He'd almost forgotten how amazing it felt to be so happy and carefree.

The moment was interrupted by a sharp shout. Finn jumped when a voice called to him from the street. He'd been so caught up in the laughter over a silly word that he hadn't noticed the sleek black car coming to a stop in front of his home. He peered across the yard at the car, one he'd heard described before as a "rich bitch" car by his mom.

"Hi there, son," the passenger called again. She was an older lady with gray-blonde hair and big sunglasses covering most of her face.

Some weird lady is here and wants to talk to me. Finn quickly composed himself, telling Snow to wait while he assessed the situation. He knew what strangers in the neighborhood meant. Strangers weren't welcome, and this particular stranger angered Finn for ruining his happy moment with Snow.

Her hand lifted, gesturing for him to approach the car. Unsure, Finn glanced back at the door then over to the car, figuring his mother wouldn't appreciate him barging in

just yet, so he had a few more minutes to spare. He saun-
tered over until he was mere inches away, hands in his
pockets gripping his carving and knife. "Sup?"

The lady removed her sunglasses. Her eyes were a
bright green, friendly and searching his face for something
he couldn't identify. Finn saw the lines around them when
she smiled. Next to her was a man probably just as old as
she was, with all-gray hair and wearing a nice suit. The
man didn't look quiet as friendly, even though he tried, but
there was a sternness to him Finn didn't like.

"We were hoping to track down our daughter and
grandson. Where can we find Annette?" the older woman
asked.

Finn nodded, suddenly tired as the effects of his mystery drink began to wear off. "Yeah. I know the lady. Got a
green trailer with a flag on it." He crossed his arms and
narrowed his eyes as a thought occurred to him. "She's got
a lot of problems. She ain't a nice lady, but ain't her fault
people keep giving her all those things to smoke. You got
a nice car. How come you got all this money and don't
help out a lady that's your daughter?"

If his question offended the pair, they didn't show it.
Instead, the woman merely smiled sadly and placed a hand
on the open windowsill. The gesture made the boy take a
step back. "Well, young man, sometimes people don't
want help, or are too proud to accept it when it's offered.
And some people don't realize when help is right in front
of them." At his frown, she reached out and bopped him
on the nose. "You'll understand one day."

Finn shrugged, then glanced over his shoulder when a
scream pierced the air. He sighed, embarrassed by what he
knew was happening inside his home. The whole neigh-

borhood knew, as he was so often reminded. Just thinking about the shame she'd caused him over the years exhausted him.

"Are you okay here, son?" the man finally spoke, looking over his wife at the boy standing forlornly on the dead grass.

His back straightened at that even as he fought a yawn. "I'm fine," Finn replied tersely.

"You'd tell us if you needed help, right?"

Finn clenched his jaw and rolled his eyes. "Why would I tell you people? I take care of myself."

The older lady only smiled a sad smile and handed him something. Hoping it was money, Finn snatched it from her hand, a little annoyed it was just a business card. "What do I need this for?"

"Whenever you need us, you call us, okay?"

He eyed the card, confused. "Why would you help me? I ain't your son, lady."

"You don't have to be blood to show someone kindness, young man."

For a reason, the response unnerved him. He didn't like people acting like he couldn't take care of himself, like he was just some dumb kid with a mom who made those screaming sounds all times of the day and night. "I don't need no help," Finn spat out, then turned on his heel and stomped back to the front step, watching out of the corner of his eye as the car slowly pulled away, all merriment from his conversation with Snow having faded away.

Three hours later, sweat soaked from the heat and crashing from his bout of *finnergy*, Finn quietly crept inside the trailer. He was hoping to sneak into his room and get his ball, maybe even stay for a nap while he was there, and get out without having to suffer through any conversation.

Those hopes were dashed when he saw his mother and a strange man draped on the couch. A blanket covered the man's lower half, while his mom wore only a bra and underwear. Both held a drink in one hand and cigarette in the other.

It took only a second for Finn to identify the man. He'd seen him several times over the years, been pushed around by him more than once in the past as he'd stalked out of his mother's room and to the front door. Just another dealer looking for payment, one way or another.

Rolling his eyes, Finn made to move past the couch, inwardly sighing when both stirred at his presence.

"The hell you want, boy?" his mom rasped out, eyes glassy, hair a mess in a bun on the top of her head.

"My ball. I was waiting outside 'til you were done." The disgust was clear in his tone.

"Then what the hell you doing in here?" Biting back a sigh, Finn merely continued toward his room, stumbling over tears in the carpet. He stopped when he felt a hand on his arm. "I tell you you could leave? You been in my drinks?"

"No."

"Don't you lie to me!"

Finn grit his teeth together when a hand slapped across his cheek, but held his ground. This wasn't the first time she'd hit him and he knew it wouldn't be the last, but he wasn't going to run away. Instead he stared her straight in the eye, a silent challenge to do it again. In fact, he even took a step closer, just to see what she would do. He didn't used to be so brave, but he had more strength in him now.

Snow's presence gave him that strength, that courage, a constant reminder that he was never alone. Besides, he always told Snow she had to be brave, even if she couldn't be mean.

Who was he to tell her to be brave, if he wasn't always brave himself?

Their glare was broken by the man's abrupt laughter. "I like this kid," he said with a gesture at Finn. "Kid's got balls. Give 'em a few years to really toughen up and he'll have himself the run of town. Assuming he don't grow up to be a punk."

"Shut up." The words escaped Finn's mouth before he realized what he was saying. Fear crept in at his mother's gasp, the way the man's lips pressed into a thin line and a muscle worked along his jaw as he sat up and leaned closer. His hulking shoulders and wide arms looked even more menacing when paired with the glower etched across his chiseled face.

"The fuck did you just say to me?"

His heart thudded against his chest worse than the feel of those clear-liquid drinks, but still he held his ground. "I said shut up. You're just another loser *she* brought home." His head cocked in his mother's direction, though his eyes remained on the man. "She don't care about you and you don't care about her. So you don't get to talk to me."

The man eyed the boy carefully before his scowl broke into a grin. But it wasn't a proud or happy grin. This one was calculating, sneaky. He rose slowly, noting the way Finn averted his eyes when the blanket fell.

"What's the matter, punk? Jealous?"

"No," the boy sneered back. It wasn't the first time he

saw one of his mom's men fully naked. It wasn't even the first time he'd seen this particular man without pants. Such was the way of life in his mother's smoke-stained trailer. "No reason to be jealous."

Barking out a chuckle, the man dressed in a pair of faded jeans with a wide leather belt and a blue button-down shirt that, surprisingly, was in decent condition. He picked up a leather jacket. "You got balls, kid," he said to Finn. "I like that. Keep it up, and come see me at the club in a few years. We could use a kid like you. Joe, remember the name."

"I'll never forget," was his quiet response, but it went unheard. Finn caught the leather jacket when it was tossed his way. He glanced down at it, then up at the man. "I ain't wearing your clothes."

"If you're gonna be a bad-ass, you better look the part." With that, the man turned and walked out.

Silence dominated the trailer after the sound of a rev-ving engine finally faded down the street. Left without the buffer of a heavily muscled dealer, Finn risked a glance at his mom, relieved to see that she was passed out on the couch, drink tipped over on the floor.

Shaking his head, he tiptoed to his room and shut the door, relieved to at least have one moment of privacy. He dragged a chair over to his makeshift dresser and stood on it, peering down at the jacket and debating with himself. He didn't want to wear it, didn't want to acknowledge what doing so would mean for him and his future. The jacket was dirty in more ways than one. And, yet, some-thing called for him to slip it on, so he did, staring at him-self in the cracked mirror. It was too big, the sleeves hang-ing past his hands and the rest of it all but engulfing his skinny frame, but in that moment, something inside Finn changed.

He wasn't going to do what his mother said anymore. He wasn't going to sit outside in the sun while she brought home men. He wasn't going to let her hit him without hitting her back.

He was going to be a bad-ass.

Snow peered through the open doorway of a newly decorated room, both amazed and horrified by what she saw—amazed by how pretty all the pinks and purples were of her bed and curtains and stuffed animals, horrified by what this new room meant for her.

When her parents sat her down and explained that she and her sister Amelia were going to get their own rooms, that they would be sleeping separately each night but only just down the hall from one another, Snow hadn't really let herself consider what that meant. She knew her old room had too much stuff in it, of course—her mommy always complained their toy chest was bursting at the seams—but it wasn't until she was standing in the doorway of her new room that the truth sunk in.

She would have to sleep alone for the first time ever.

Years ago, when she was first adopted, the lady at the group home had told her she was getting a new sister, a real sister who would love her and want to be best friends. Snow wouldn't have to share a big room with lots of other girls who didn't like one another. No, now she was getting a friend, a whole family. What did it mean, then, that her sister didn't want to live with her anymore?

"Honey, what are you doing?"

Snow jumped and instantly backed away from the door. She felt guilty, but wasn't sure why, as her father knelt down to her level. "Just looking," she whispered, pointing one small hand inside the room.

Her father smiled. "What do you think of your new room? Did you like getting to pick all your new decorations?" When Snow only shrugged, he frowned. "What's the matter, honey?"

Taking in a deep breath, Snow looked over at her bed, her pretty white dresser with a music box and mermaid lamp, then back at her dad. "I think it is beautiful. But..."

"But what?"

"Do you and Mommy and Amelia still love me and want to live with me?" Her woeful blue eyes looked up at her father's brown ones, their appearances completely opposite but concerned expressions matching.

"Oh, honey." He gathered her in his arms and offered her a tender embrace, one hand patting her back in a comforting way he'd done since the day they brought her home. Once Snow seemed appeased, he pulled back and looked at her, his expression serious. "Of course we love you and want to live with you. We love you and your sister both the same amount. You will always be our little girls and nothing will ever change that. You get your own room because you're going to be a big girl someday, and you can have all this space just for you and your friends. Okay?"

Snow sniffled and nodded, resting her head on his shoulder. Indeed, she knew this man was her daddy and that he loved her, but sometimes the words *pet store* still ran through her mind.

Are you sad, Snow?

Her face buried in her father's arms, Snow smiled. *Not anymore*, she told Finn, happy to hear his voice, comforted by her father's embrace. She told him about her new room, about her father's assurance that she was still loved.

Good for you.

She heard the bitterness in his reply, wondered about it. Something had changed in Finn recently. She didn't know what, but she could feel it, hear it in his words. Sometimes he was nice and funny and happy, other days he was almost mad. Never at her, just ... at life, she surmised.

Why are you moving rooms?

So me and my sister will have lots of space for us and our friends.

You have a sister?

Snow frowned, sure she'd told Finn all about Amelia. Going over their conversations, she wondered how she could have forgotten to talk about her sister all these years, though deep down she guessed it was because she wanted her friend all for herself. If Finn knew about Amelia, he might want to talk to her too. Everyone loved talking to Amelia and being friends with her.

Yeah ... her name's Amelia. She's one year older. It dawned on her only after the admission that she'd just revealed her sister's name, when she'd been so careful to avoid giving her own. But lots of people were named Amelia, and surely Finn wouldn't be able to use one name to find out *her* real name.

Not commenting on the little piece of truth, Finn asked, *What's she look like?*

With an internal shrug, Snow pictured her sister in her

mind. *I don't know. Pretty. Her hair is pretty and dark and long and looks like Daddy's. She's really skinny 'cause she is in dance class.*

Is she a good big sister?

Yes. Snow loved her sister, as different as they were. *She's awesome. She doesn't like to play dolls or dress-up or watch cartoons with me, but she's still really fun.*

I bet you're a good little sister.

Snow smiled at Finn's proclamation, no doubt made to make up for his earlier snap. *I bet if your mom has more kids you'll be a good big brother.*

Finn hesitated at the admission, then replied, *Nope. I like to get into trouble.*

You have to stay away from trouble, Finn. You have to be good, so we can be friends.

We'll always be friends, he insisted, and Snow could almost feel the smile he wore. *I get into trouble so you don't have to, remember?*

She did remember. Finn had told her all kinds of stories about all kinds of trouble, fights he'd gotten into and arguments with grownups. While she'd laughed with him at the time, now the stories worried her, because she didn't want to give Finn up if it meant being a good person.

Snow? he asked after a few minutes had passed. *You ever gonna tell me your real name?*

She thought about it before answering. Her parents had warned her about strangers and how important it was to never tell anyone she'd never met before her name or where she lived. The policemen could be trusted, and her teachers at school, and the people she knew were family members.

But Finn was none of those things. He was a friend,

her very best friend, but he was not on the list of people her parents approved of as "not strangers." And, even though she desperately wanted to reveal herself to Finn, something held her back—a conversation she'd heard as a little girl that was never meant for her ears.

She'd been playing in her room just after she was adopted, enjoying her new dolls and spending hours making them look beautiful in their fancy dresses and shoes. When she was finally sleepy and ready for bed, she'd crept to her new parents' bedroom, about to knock, but the words escaping the cracked door made her pause.

"This is dangerous," her mother was saying. *"These people are mad at you. They aren't good people."*

"I know," her father had agreed. *"But this is my job, honey. It's my job to put these bad people away so they can't hurt anyone else."*

"But you are trusting the wrong people to give you information. What if they turn on you? You never know if it's a trap." A long moment of whispered words before her voice raised again. *"We have children now. It's not like when we were in our early twenties and the whole idea of justice and beating the bad guys was this grand dream. What if they try to retaliate? Come after us? They have threatened you before, and—"*

"We can't let them win," her daddy had cut in, softly but sternly. *"They will always threaten us, because that's what they do. They're criminals. But I can't stop doing what I do out of fear, and I have to get information where I can if it means putting other bad guys away for good. We can, and will, protect our children. They are smart. They know not to talk to strangers. We'll do what we can to make sure they always know strangers can be dangerous."*

At the time, and even now, Snow didn't fully understand the entire conversation. But what she did understand
was that someone, some stranger who was not a good person, might one day try to do something bad. She loved her
parents and her house and her family, and didn't want to
go away with someone who wasn't a good person. That
fear stayed with her each and every day, wondering what
would happen if she chose the wrong person to trust. No
one could know her name unless her parents said it was
okay.

She finally answered Finn on a sigh, *Maybe someday.*

*But I want to know now. Maybe I'll just tell you my
real name and then you'll have to tell me yours.*

Don't. The single word was filled with urgency because she knew she'd have to do just that.

*Maybe I want to. Maybe I should just say it. My name
is—*

STOP! So urgent and forceful was her reply that
Snow jumped, causing her father to pull back with a concerned frown. *Finn, if you tell me then I'm not talking to
you anymore.*

"Is something wrong?" her father asked, at the same
time Finn said sulkily, *Fine. I'll just be Finn then.*

Thank you. Satisfied, Snow looked up at her dad.
"I'm okay. I ... thought a bug was on me."

"Goofball." Her father straightened and held out a
hand. "Come on, princess, let's go get some dinner!"

Together they ran down the hall, Snow giggling when
her father pretended to trip, letting her win the race to the
kitchen table. Her giggles matched her sister's as they both
wrestled with their daddy and argued over who got the
most chocolate milk, their mother glancing over her shoul-

der every so often with a smile on her face.

"Dinnertime!" her mother said, picking up a casserole dish and placing it in the center of the table. At the same time, her father set down plates and piled them high with lasagna. Snow wasted no time digging in to her favorite meal, doing her best not to get sauce all over herself and the tablecloth.

"So," her dad said after a few minutes of eating. "Rumor has it someone at this table has a birthday coming up." Snow's ears perked up at that. "It wouldn't be a certain little girl turning eleven years old, would it?"

"Yes!" she cried with a grin. "I will be!"

Her mom laughed. "What would you like to do for your birthday? We can go to your favorite restaurant and a movie, or maybe have a party and invite all of your friends."

"Princess party!" Snow cried again, sending a wide grin over to Amelia when she made a gagging sound. Her sister didn't like girly stuff, preferring sports over dolls and blues over pinks, but a princess party sounded thrilling to Snow, especially since she finally had friends at school who didn't make fun of her for being adopted.

"A princess party sounds just perfect," her father agreed. "Balloons, maybe a piñata, a big cake, and oh the presents! We can't forget those!"

"Presents!" Snow echoed, stabbing a bite of lasagna. "Can I invite Finn?" she asked before shoving the pasta in her mouth. So consumed in the food, she didn't notice the quick look of concern her mother shot her dad.

"Finn?" her mom repeated after a pause. "You still talk to Finn?"

Feeling as though she'd done something wrong, Snow

dropped her hands to her lap and looked down. The weight of her parents' stares bore down on her, flooding her with worry. "I'm sorry," she said, not sure why, but feeling that was the right thing to say. "Am I not supposed to be friends with him?"

"It's just fine that you are friends," her dad said before her mom could reply. His eyes held a message Snow couldn't read, but wasn't meant for her anyway. "But Finn hasn't told you any more mean things to say, right?"

"No," Snow promised. "We just talk about regular stuff. I told him about my new room. He told me about his mom and how she's not very nice to him."

Her mom shifted in her seat, catching her husband's quick head shake across the table. "And where do you talk to Finn, sweetie?"

Snow pointed to her forehead. "In my mind."

"Do you ... do you ever see him?"

"Like in person?" Snow's face scrunched up as she thought. "Nope, only in my head. I don't know what he looks like or what his real name is."

When her parents didn't answer, instead simply smiling over at her, Snow went back to her lasagna, but couldn't stop feeling like she'd done something wrong.

CHAPTER 5

T HE NEXT MORNING, Snow made her way downstairs to the living room, eager to watch her favorite Saturday movie before her parents made her go grocery shopping with them, and other weekend chores she found boring. After finding the DVD she wanted and putting it in the player like her daddy showed her to, she snuggled up on the couch with a soft pillow and even softer blanket.

Halfway into the movie, the doorbell rang. Snow ignored it, as well as her mother greeting their company, attention entirely transfixed on the princess dancing with animals on the screen. She stirred only when footsteps sounded next to the couch. Glancing behind her, Snow saw her mom with a lady who looked a lot younger. Both were smiling.

"Honey, this is Miss Jenn. Come say hi?"

Barely turning her eyes away from the TV, Snow offered a quick greeting over her shoulder. "Hi."

"I'm going to get us something to drink," her mom said, seemingly irritated by her daughter's flippant response. "Have a seat, Miss Jenn."

Miss Jenn entered the room, taking a seat on the couch, next to where Snow rested. A bit curious now, Snow glanced over, interested to see that the other lady was not only younger than her mom, but also wore a lot more makeup and dressed much differently. Her mom was gentle and soft and wore colors like the earth. This new lady had bright-red hair cut short around her face and dark-brown eyes surrounded by thin lines of black and smudges of blue that made her look a little sparkly. Her face was lightly freckled and friendly, as cheerful as the light-blue dress she wore that floated around her knees like a cloud.

Snow liked her instantly.

"What are you watching?" Miss Jenn asked with a smile.

"*Snow White*," Snow replied absently, looking back at the TV. "Mommy and Daddy bought me the movie when I came to live with them 'cause it's my favorite."

"That was nice of them. I used to watch *Snow White* all the time when I was your age," Miss Jess replied, shifting so she was half facing Snow. "Do you mind if I watch with you?"

"Kay." Snow offered her a blanket, which Miss Jenn accepted, laying it across her lap. They both turned back to the movie, watching in silence together.

Snow had almost forgotten the lady was there when she asked, "Doesn't Amelia want to watch the movie?"

"She doesn't like cartoon movies. She watches boy

shows and doesn't like the same things I do."

"That's too bad," Miss Jenn mused. "Do you ever get to watch *Snow White* with your friends?"

"I watch and tell Finn about it sometimes." The answer escaped before she realized she might have said something wrong. But Miss Jenn only smiled again.

"That's nice. Everyone should have friends to watch movies with, right?" When Snow nodded, the older woman continued, "Does Finn go to your school?"

Snow hesitated, worry creeping into her mind — and that hesitation was all the boy on the other end of her thoughts needed.

What's wrong?

Snow felt herself retreat into her mind, soothed by Finn's question, by the fact that he could sense her discomfort. Though they hadn't learned to recognize the good feelings and times of happiness, it was enough that they could find one another when a friend was truly needed.

There's a lady here who asked me about you, she answered Finn.

Who is she?

I don't know. Mommy's friend. Snow chewed on her bottom lip as Miss Jenn looked down at her with a soft expression, saying her name twice before the child finally glanced up.

"Is Finn a boy from your school, maybe in your class?" she repeated. "Has he ever come over to your house to play or watch movies?"

She wants to know if you're from my school and if you ever come over, she told Finn.

The words *Don't tell her nothing!* rang through her head just as Miss Jenn asked, "Are you okay, sweetie?"

Finn said something else, but his protests were drowned out by Miss Jenn. "Are you talking to him right now?"

She asked if I'm talking to you right now.

Tell her no.

But that's a lie. She heard Finn sigh in her head, but he didn't say anything else. *Finn? Finn?*

"Sweetie, are you talking to him right now?"

Snow frowned and shook her head. "No," she answered honestly, wondering if he'd left so she wouldn't have to lie. She really wasn't talking to him, but she could feel him inside her mind, her heart, waiting until he could come back out and talk.

"Who is Finn?"

"Just … a boy in a movie I saw." That much was true.

"Do you like pretending Finn is your friend?"

She wasn't pretending, but didn't want this new person to know that. So instead Snow replied, "I guess."

"Why do you like to pretend talk to Finn?"

This was a question she could answer. "When I first came here I didn't have lots of friends. They called me mean names at school. Finn was my friend and was nice to me, and helped me when I was sad."

"Kids can be very cruel," Miss Jenn agreed. "I'm glad you had a friend to help you when all the kids at school weren't being nice to you. And what about now? Do you have friends at school?"

Thinking back to all the girls and boys in her class, Snow shrugged. "Some. Amelia has lots more."

"Some friends can be just as good as lots of friends." Miss Jenn nudged Snow with her shoulder playfully, trying to get the girl's fallen face to perk up. "Now that you have new friends, do you still talk to Finn? Even as just pretend?"

The lie was on the tip of her tongue, but Snow was unable to speak it. Her young mind struggled to come up with a way to answer the question without giving away the truth. Carefully, Snow replied, "I like to say things in my head when people are mean or I'm scared."

When Miss Jenn smiled and patted her leg, Snow figured she'd said something right. She flicked her gaze back to the movie, pleased that no more questions were asked. A few minutes later Miss Jenn got up and walked to the kitchen, speaking quietly with Snow's mom. Snow couldn't hear what was said, but did know one thing after this strange conversation with a mystery lady.

From now on, Finn would be her little secret.

Finn wandered around the convenience store, sneakily tracking his mother's progress. It had been a happy coincidence that she'd already been in the store when he entered on his way home from a trip to his graveyard garden—happy only because he knew with her there, walking out with some snacks under his jacket was going to be so much easier.

From behind a rack of chips, he watched her grab her usual stock of vodka, cigarettes, and beer. The scent of corn nuts and pork rinds hit him from the bags by his head, making his stomach rumble and reminding him he hadn't eaten since last night.

The grating sound of his mother's hoarse laughter had him shaking his head and slipping down the farthest aisle to get away from the racket. After grabbing a bag of chips, of course, tucking it beneath the leather jacket and sniffling in attempt to hide the crinkling sound. Another laugh had him grabbing a pack of gum. His mother was likely flirting with the cashier to get free cigarettes. She did that a lot. When flirting didn't work, she convinced them to disappear into the back room for a few minutes. For a long time he didn't know what she actually did when that happened to score her free stuff, until talk around town clued him in to her actions.

When he saw her leading the cashier, a middle-aged man with a beer gut and a gold band on his left ring finger, down the hallway behind the beer coolers, he knew it would be one of those days and rolled his eyes. He'd learned not to be ashamed of his mother, just disappointed, and instead trash talked her just as much as the other kids and adults did behind her back. It was easier that way.

While both parent and cashier were distracted, Finn took the opportunity to sneak a few candy bars, a small bag of chips, a bottle of Coke, and a single serving of cereal into his pockets. He wore the too-large leather jacket given to him by his mom's long-past fling, and the size gave him plenty of room to conceal his goods. Before the cashier returned he waltzed outside and found his mother's car, deciding it was easier to catch a ride home than walk in the heat. He'd tear into those snacks when he was alone in his room. Otherwise *she* would take them for herself.

His mother appeared a few moments later, bags in hand. He doubted she'd paid for any of her items either. Not with money, anyway. "Where'd you come from?" she asked when she dropped into the driver's seat and lit a cigarette.

"Around," he answered vaguely, knowing she

wouldn't question his whereabouts. It was their arrange-
ment. He didn't ask about her men, she didn't care what he
did all day.

"Whatever." When she pulled out on the street, opposite direction of home, he sat up a little straighter.

"Where are you going?"

"Have a stop to make. It won't take long."

"I want to go home."

"Then you shouldn't have come along."

Finn slumped back against the seat and stewed silently as his mom made the drive to the edge of town. He recognized the neighborhood only by stories he'd heard told
by others. It wasn't quite as bad as his own trailer park, but
it wasn't a place he'd be all too happy to see at night, either. Graffiti covered the sides of buildings and shops were
locked behind barred windows. What few cars were
parked on the side of the road were in worse condition
than his mother's own beat-up vehicle. Up ahead was a
building that looked to Finn like a bar or club. It sat
against a backdrop of old warehouses and was wrapped in
blacked-out windows to protect it from prying eyes.

She pulled up next to that building where nothing
good could possibly happen, its neon lights flashing in the
growing dusk. Without a word to her son, she hopped out
and strolled inside, taking the keys with her. Not wanting
any part of whatever would go down in that place, Finn
stayed put, deciding to enjoy his pilfered treats while he
still could.

When his food was gone and boredom set in, Finn sat
back and stared at the building's front door. Above it, red-
dish-blue letters spelled out the word *Infinity*. Inside he
knew he'd find the city's most infamous names, including

one of his mother's visitors—and the man who gave him his leather jacket. But no one had gone in or out since his mother, and he was starting to wonder if she'd slipped out the back and left him there.

Hoping for the best, he started rooting around the car in search of entertainment, finding it in the form of a random copper wire. Already seeing its potential, he began to shape the thin metal, looping a head, bending legs, twisting and tying a piece of his candy wrapper to form clothes. When he was done he had a tiny man two inches tall, with one arm slightly longer than the other.

"No one's perfect," he told the figure, deciding not to fix it. A glance out the window showed him the doors were still closed, the sidewalks empty. "Bet you wouldn't let a lady like that take you to the back room," he said to the man, imagining him nodding back. "Bet you're better than that. *I'll* be better than that."

When he went to move the man to the dashboard, ready to imagine him having a normal, happy morning with family, Finn felt a rush of worry, making his arms hesitate in the air. By now he recognized it not as his own worry, but belonging to the girl who didn't know how to handle such emotions.

What's wrong? he asked Snow, already poised to help her defend herself. But, instead of bullies at school, she told him about a lady at her house asking about him, a friend of her mommy's who wanted to know if he was in Snow's class.

Don't tell her nothing! was his immediate response, now feeling his own worry that their secret was being revealed. He knew how scared Snow was of strangers and respected her wishes to keep their real names and homes separate—so who was this lady who knew about him, and would she make Snow stop talking to him?

She asked if I'm talking to you right now.

Finn sat up straighter, instantly mad at the fact some person thought she could butt into his friendship with Snow. His anger forced out a reply to sound as harsh and serious as possible. *Tell her no.*

But that's a lie.

"What's so wrong with lying?" he muttered to himself, half annoyed by her unwillingness to say anything that wasn't the truth. If she wouldn't lie, then he could at least make it so she wouldn't have to. So he sat with his arms crossed and pouted rather than say anything else.

Finn?

He heard her calling and debated answering. If there was a lady asking about him on the other end of their conversation, then Finn didn't want her knowing anything else. And, he figured, if he stopped answering, then Snow could tell the truth. So he stayed silent, hating how much it hurt to ignore Snow's attempts to contact him in a moment of need, feeling like he was betraying her. It felt like a hand reaching into his body and pulling him forward. But still he resisted, closing his eyes against the pain of silencing his own voice.

After a few long minutes the internal tugging began to fade. Finn released a breath, grateful Snow was no longer in need yet wondering what had happened. He considered asking her, but didn't want to risk the woman still being there. Instead he returned his attention back to the wire man, and continued his wait.

AN HOUR LATER his mother emerged, one side of her face bruised and her hair a mess. "What happened to you?" he asked, half curious, half not caring. He was sure that whatever it was, she probably earned it one way or another.

"Mind your own business," she snapped, peeling out of the parking lot and steering the car toward home.

He couldn't help the snide comment that escaped next. "Owe more money?" At the tears in her eyes, he felt a strange stirring of sympathy and found himself softening. Even after all the terrible things she'd done, when she cried it made him feel guilty. "You could ask—"

"Shut up!" his mother shouted, swerving to the side of the road and stomping on the brakes. Finn barely had a second to catch himself before she grabbed hold of his collar and pulled him over until they were face to face. "You listen here, and don't make me tell you again. We don't ask for help. We are better than that. You got that, you little shit?"

His face a portrait of indifference, Finn nodded. But it wasn't enough for her, and she all but snarled in his face, shoving him hard against the seat and swatting the metal man in his hand. It tumbled to the floor. "And why do you make these stupid things? Get you nowhere in life. Grow up and do something useful for once, will you?"

Retrieving the figure, Finn chose not to answer, not trusting his voice not to waver with the sadness burning in his throat. Slightly trembling fingers smoothed out dents in the wire to reshape the man's head. He liked making them because it was the only thing in the whole world he was good at, and they distracted him from the suckiness that was his real life. But he would never admit that to anyone.

Well, except maybe Snow.

When his mother sighed and focused again on the road, Finn adjusted his jacket and turned his head to look out the window. Accepting her hate, her miserable outlook on the world, was harder to bear these days. And now he couldn't even talk to Snow about it.

Tears threatened to build. Finn shoved them back, angry at his own weakness, and stared at the club retreating in the side mirror.

"*You got balls, kid,*" Joe had said to him that day he dared to talk back to one of the toughest men in town.

"*Come see me at the club in a few years,*" had been his invitation, a summons to a specific place at an unspecific time for reasons unknown.

"*Joe, remember the name.*" A name Finn had already known, a name he would never, ever, forget.

As his mother turned down the street he'd grown up on, Finn told himself it was time to stop crying and time to stop letting his mom make him feel bad. He had to toughen up, forget the past and how he'd let people push him around as a kid. He had to grow up—and growing up meant focusing on the future, doing whatever he had to do to prepare for it.

Joe was waiting for him.

CHAPTER 6

EXHAUSTED, SNOW FELL into the recliner, watching her four-year-old neighbor run around the living room using a blanket as a cape as she pretended to be a superhero. At thirteen, Snow considered herself pretty fun and full of energy, but she couldn't keep up with the kid, especially when she was left alone to babysit while both sets of parents went out to dinner to celebrate some kind of "big win," as her dad put it. And especially when her sister chose to spend the night hiding in her room instead of helping out.

"I wanna play!" the child insisted, holding out a doll and abandoning the cape.

"Bedtime," Snow insisted. The girl's face scrunched into what Snow recognized as a look of evil determination.

"You have to play or I'll tell Mommy you were mean to me," was the garbled reply, spoken in childish gibberish with just the right amount of manipulation to have Snow quickly jumping to her feet.

"Okay, okay. Ten minutes of playtime, then bed."

"I win!" the little girl cheered, grabbing another doll and plunking down on the carpet. "Wanna play dolls?" When Snow didn't immediately answer, she screeched, "Wanna play dolls?!"

Unable to resist, Snow replied with a nod then silently shouted, *FINN WANNA PLAY DOLLS?*

The reply came quickly. *You scared the shit out of me.*

Snow laughed both aloud and so he could hear. Over the past few years they'd gotten better at talking to one another at random times, often without having to even concentrate on sending their thoughts. It didn't always work, but at least they didn't need to be sad or scared to find each other anymore.

Watch your language, young man.

Yeah, yeah.

Finn had gotten used to Snow lecturing him on his worsening mouth. She knew his language was a product of his environment and how he was raised. Not that she knew all the details, just that he lived in a bad area and his mom was a pretty terrible person. She knew he got in trouble a lot, and had been suspended from school last year for fighting. But despite all that, how she felt about him never changed. He was her best friend, even if no one knew about him.

She'd never broken her promise to herself, and kept Finn a secret after Miss Jenn's visit ... and second and third and fourth visits after that. It made her parents happy that she no longer talked to Finn, and it made her happy to keep talking to him, so keeping her secret was the best choice for everyone.

Why are you playing dolls anyway? Aren't you supposed to be too old for that now?

The question broke her out of her thoughts. *You're never too old to play with dolls.*

Pretty sure that's not true.

It is, she insisted playfully, then added with a grin, *It's totally finntertaining.*

Even in his head he groaned at the bad joke. *Dork.*

You're just jealous you can't come up with anything for Snow.

Yeah, yeah. So you're not seriously playing with dolls are you? Like by yourself?

Snow filled him in on her babysitting job, then moved on to updates about her life since it had been a couple weeks since they last talked. Funny school stories, nice things her parents did for her. She no longer feared they would stop loving her or want to give her back, but Snow still tried hard to be the best daughter possible.

Babies are lame. I never want any.

Snow huffed. *Babies are fun. I want a bunch when I grow up and get married.*

'Cause you're a girl, and girls are mushy.

Yeah well, you're a boy. And boys are so FINNicky. Snow giggled to herself and imagined him rolling his eyes. She'd learned the word last week and couldn't wait to use it with him. Even better was getting to use a second pun so quickly in conversation.

You really are such a nerd, Finn replied with a laugh, then fell silent.

Having grown used to long lapses in conversation, Snow turned back to the little girl at her feet, acting out an entire wedding scene with her before Finn finally popped back into her thoughts like a flicker of light behind her eyes. When he did, his voice was hesitant, questioning.

Snow, you think that sometimes it's okay to do bad things? Like, maybe it's not a bad thing if it's for a good reason?

The question worried her. *Depends on what you're doing, I guess. And why you're doing it. Why? What are you doing?*

The sun had long since lowered by the time Finn finally reached his destination. Hands in his pockets to ward off the chill in the evening air, he stared from the corner at the nondescript building lit up by a single light in the parking lot and flashing neon bulbs coming from inside. He'd only seen the outside of the club during the day, never at night, never quite able to tell exactly what lay in wait for him inside.

He'd snuck out of the house before dinner, hitching a ride until he could make the rest of his way across town on foot. Finn knew he would be in trouble later, but didn't care. This was the moment he'd been planning for years, ever since he'd decided to grow up and get what he wanted out of life. The day he'd no longer be the boy hiding in the closet, but the bad-ass he was meant to be.

The following years had been filled with preparation. He'd exercised, got in fights so people knew not to mess with him, listened to talk on the streets for names he needed to know, even stole alcohol and cigarettes when he could so he didn't look like a rookie if it was offered when he walked into the club.

For a fleeting moment, Finn wondered what Snow would think of him, standing on the street corner surrounded by run-down homes and trash lining the gutters, with only neon lights guiding him to an uncertain future. He could easily see her doing something *good*, something boring, while he was about to walk into the darkest part of his town. But then he decided he didn't care.

He was thirteen now, old enough to make up his own mind. He was doing this, and he was doing this now.

FINN WANNA PLAY DOLLS?

Snow's outburst startled him back onto the curb just as he'd started crossing the street. Heart thumping—part caught off-guard by his friend, part nervous about what he was about to do—Finn allowed himself a moment to reply only because it had been a while since they last spoke.

The conversation nearly unnerved him. It was so innocent, her thoughts filled with so much joy and her replies so playful, Snow actually listening when he gave her a brief recap of his life. If only she could have been there with him, next to him, guiding him to a path where they could always be friends.

What are you doing?

The question rang loud and clear in his head. Remembering where he was, who was and wasn't by his side, Finn took a moment to decide how he wanted to answer it. He didn't want to say anything at all, because he'd made a promise to himself a long time ago never to lie to his only real friend, so instead he quickly said, *Don't worry about it, I was just asking*, and ended the conversation.

Alone in his thoughts now, he pushed Snow's subconscious to the back of his own and forced himself to hold his head high. Across the street awaited his destination, beckoning to him, inviting him in from the cold. Normally Finn loved the winter air and all the brilliant white snow that came with it—winter made everyone even, didn't care who it fell upon, who it froze; in the dead of winter, no one was tougher than nature—but tonight he wanted nothing more than to give in to the lure of warmth.

He continue the trek to the club, until he was facing the back door. Club Infinity was one of the more popular hangouts in town even though it was never promoted around town like other companies, but everyone knew the place for what it was. There was a reason the club was one of the few businesses in the area that managed to stay open for any length of time. Drugs, gambling, women. Taking care of the competition so no other name except Infinity was spoken. Paying off cops and city officials to look the other way. As far as Finn knew, there was no limit.

And now he was ready to make a profit, too.

Finn squared his shoulders and knocked hard on reinforced steel, a demand to be answered. When the door opened he had to force himself not to take a step back. In front of him stood a tall, bald man with bulging muscles so large he barely fit in the doorway, glaring down at him behind a pair of dark sunglasses that hid his eyes, but not his scowl.

"What do you want?"

Finn made sure his face matched the man's expression as he replied, "I wanna see Joe."

The man scoffed. "Ain't nobody sees Joe 'less Joe wants to be seen. You know you can't come in here, kid." He made to close the door, but Finn slammed a hand on the hard metal. Though he wasn't strong enough to actually stop the man, he did succeed in catching his attention.

"I know who you are, Chix. And I know Joe is here. So, Chix, I wanna see Joe and you ain't gonna stop me."

The man paused and finally took a good, long look at the teenager in front of him. "You wearin' Joe's old jacket?"

Finn adjusted the leather jacket, which was still too big, and nodded. He got that question a lot because of the red infinity symbol stitched at the right shoulder. He always assumed it was the club's logo, especially since other people knew it as Joe's, though the symbol was nowhere to be found on the club's sign or building. "He gave it to me. Said to come see him when I was ready."

Chix grinned at that, revealing two rows of crooked white teeth. "Did he now? Come on in then, kid. Let's see what good old Joe has to say about that."

Breathing deep, Finn stepped out of the cold and into the black hole of Infinity. Instantly he was swallowed in a world of red—red lights, red walls, red chair just inside the back door. As he followed the large man down the hall, he felt Snow pricking at the corners of his mind, trying to find out what he was doing, but he pushed her back.

She didn't need to know about this.

CHAPTER

7

H E STOOD ON the other side of a massive wooden desk. The sides and surface were scarred with age and abuse despite the sleek and smooth coating, the wood faded, the top bare save for a lamp, pack of cigarettes, and laptop. And behind the desk were two men, one sitting in a large leather chair, the other standing at his side with his arms crossed.

The one who stood was a man Finn hadn't spoken to in almost three years, but saw here and there around town. Once he'd watched from a distance as the man stomped out of his trailer only a few weeks after catching him on the couch with his mother. Finn never forgot his name— Joe—though he had forgotten how intimidating the man was. Tall, narrowed brown eyes, with huge shoulders and a broad, scowling face accented by a scar along his jaw, Joe was every bit the kind of angry bad guy people expected to be in Club Infinity.

But Joe was nothing compared to the calm and collected man in a tailored black suit who sat before him. He was older, old enough to be his grandfather, with gray hair perfectly styled in slicked-back strands and eyes so blue Finn felt like he was looking at ice. Indeed, his entire expression was cold, down to the purse of his lips and the rigid set of wide shoulders. He wasn't a large man, rather slim actually, but his presence exuded confidence, authority ... the assurance of certain death should anyone cross his path the wrong way.

Yes, Finn knew this man too. Everyone knew Charlie.

"Kid said he's here to see you, Joe. Said you were expecting him."

Finn had forgotten about the bouncer who let him in and was now retreating toward the door. He jumped when the voice sounded behind him, inwardly cursing himself for the slight. If they noticed, they didn't comment, instead merely staring at the boy in the oversized leather jacket wearing an expression that tried a little too hard to be tough.

Joe broke the silence after the bouncer left the office, closing the door behind him. "So that's where my jacket ran off to."

The greeting confused and disappointed Finn. He dropped his backpack to the floor and crossed his arms, torn between being offended or pissed off that Joe was looking at him like he was just another kid on the street. "You saying you don't remember me?"

Joe laughed. It was a hoarse sound, grating, every bit as rough as the man it belonged to. "Yeah, yeah. I remember you. Kid with balls of steel," he replied with a dismissive shrug. "How's your momma?"

Finn's jaw clenched at the question and humiliation burned his cheeks. It was no secret to anyone in the room that his mom had more than one encounter with Joe. Just as it was no secret she had more than one encounter with most of the men in town. Even though he'd learned to turn the other cheek to people's snarky comments, it still burned when they threw her choices in his face. It wasn't his fault she spread her legs as soon as someone came to the door with coke in their hands.

"Fine." His eventual response was clipped and bitter.

Joe only laughed again. "Don't get mad at me, punk. I ain't the one offering the whole town open access."

"You're just the one demanding that access."

For the first time since Finn entered the room, the man at the desk seemed to notice him. He chuckled, a deep and almost friendly sound, even as Joe smirked. "Your momma wants the goods," he replied nonchalantly, "so I take her goods in return. That's business."

"You ain't a businessman. You're just a lackey," Finn shot back.

"Now look here, you little—"

"Enough, Joe," the man in charge silenced with a wave of a manicured and gold-ringed hand. "Are you really arguing with a child over sleeping with his mother?" He grabbed a cigarette from the pack on the desk and lit it, taking a long drag while observing the teenage boy. In the harsh light of the office Finn felt small and exposed, and hated it.

"So," Charlie drawled, those piercing blue eyes seeing right through the boy, "Joe gives you his jacket and you think that makes you just like him, huh?"

"No."

"No? Then what does it make you?"

Caught, Finn had to think about the question. What *did* the jacket make him? The wrong answer would have him kicked out on his ass in a heartbeat. The right answer would give him exactly what he wanted. Charlie waited patiently, fingers tapping lightly against one another.

Finally Finn straightened his shoulders and said, "It makes me just what you need. I don't wanna be like Joe. I want to be better."

"Better," Charlie mused, sparing a quick glance at Joe and seeing his second hand torn between amusement and rage. "Better sounds interesting. But I don't need better. I need best."

"Good, 'cause that's what I am." He was glad his comeback sounded far stronger than he felt on the inside.

"The best, huh. Little teenage boy with no experience and no real knowledge of the world is the best to ever walk into my office. Should I bow in your presence?" Lifting a brow, he held out the pack of cigarettes, both an offering and a test.

Cautiously, Finn reached out and took one, holding it with confidence when Charlie reached over with the lighter. He'd seen his mother smoke hundreds of times and tried his own hand at it over the years for specifically this moment. Here, he had something to prove.

Despite all his practice, Finn's throat and chest burned with the first drag, and he fought a cough as he released a breath in a cloud of smoke. A bitter, disgusting taste filled his mouth but he refused to show any signs of discomfort.

Satisfied, Charlie nodded and sat back. "So, what's up, kid?"

"My name's not kid."

"No? Then what is it?"

"Finn."

Charlie shot him a look of amusement, one the boy recognized as being dismissed. He'd seen that look too many times from adults over the years. "Finn, huh?" the man at the desk repeated as Joe shook his head. "If you say so. All right, *kid*, if you want to be here and be like 'ole Joe, or be better than Joe, as you say, let's try again. What do you want?"

His answer was direct, honest. "Money."

"Money? You're barely out of diapers. What do you need money for?"

Finn took a step closer to the desk, staring the other man down. "'Cause I need it. And I know you got it. Why I need it ain't any business of yours. So you gonna give me a job or what?"

The man who could just as easily kill him as give him a job sat forward, the lamp highlighting his face in ominous shadows angled along sharp cheekbones. "Some scrawny and scraggly kid? What good is a tired and hungry kid to me?"

"So give me something to eat. See what I can do after I bulk up."

After a pause, Charlie chuckled and gestured to Joe, who gave a curt nod before disappearing into the hallway. Both boy and man were silent, Finn clenching his teeth together in an effort to keep from shuffling his feet and wringing his hands together, until Joe returned a few minutes later, tossing a burger wrapped in aluminum foil on the desk in front of Finn.

"Eat," Charlie ordered, sitting back with a sly grin

and glancing over at Joe. "Tell my old lady I'll be late tonight. We got ourselves a new recruit."

———————

Three hours later Finn stepped inside the dilapidated
trailer, hands in the deep pockets of his leather jacket. He
smelled smoke and liquor as soon as he stepped inside,
saw his mother passed out on the couch, a belt secured
around her calf since her arms were too useless for a high
anymore.

"Not wasting any time," he mumbled, not at all surprised to find her in this condition and kicking himself for
thinking that, maybe now, things would be different.

Walking right past her without bothering to make sure
she was even still alive, Finn stalked to his bedroom, closing and locking the door behind him before facing inside
and taking in the new piece of furniture. An old crib was
set up next to the bed, the paint peeling. A small whimper
came from the direction of that crib. Finn looked over at
where his little brother lay on an old mattress covered in a
thin and tattered sheet. The baby was wide awake and,
judging by the smell in the room, in need of a bath.

His baby brother was barely old enough to open his
eyes, yet already was being left to apparently care for himself. Finn couldn't believe the hospital workers let his
mother leave with an infant she clearly couldn't care for.
Then again, it wasn't like they could pass him off to the
baby's father, seeing as how no one, not even his mother,
knew just who that was. Finn wanted to hate the baby, and
indeed was so embarrassed by it that he hadn't even told
Snow his mom was pregnant and did his best not to think

about it, but instead he felt sorry for the baby.

Now this little boy, too, was stuck with their mother.

Wordlessly, Finn slid off his backpack and set it on the bed before unzipping the front pouch. He removed a wad of cash and shoved it in his jacket pockets, trying not to think of what he'd done to earn it. Though he knew deep down the packages he'd been told to deliver were full of some kind of drug, he preferred to believe he was just delivering someone's mail. It was easier to believe than accepting he was now contributing to addictions like the ones that plagued his own mother.

But it was worth it, he told himself, unpacking the rest of the bag. Soon his bed showed the rewards of his less-than-upstanding job: a new blanket to keep his brother warm, a box of diapers and wipes, a two-pack of onesies, jars of baby food he wasn't sure the infant could eat yet, bottles, and a few cans of formula the clerk at the store said a new baby could drink.

Unpeeling a banana he'd bought for himself, Finn sat down on the bed next to the crib and peered through the bars at his new little brother. He'd never seen anything so small, so helpless, so in need of protection. "Hey there. Remember me? I'm your big brother. Your mom ... our mom ... she's pretty useless. No surprise there, huh? But I'm here now. And I'll protect you."

It was a promise he'd made the very first time he saw the baby—to protect the child from all the horrors of their world in a way that was never done for him. Finn was never given a chance in his life; he'd make damn sure his brother got one. He'd take care of his brother so the police didn't come back and bring that too-friendly woman who asked too many questions, so no one ever hurt him and took away all the things he loved most. He may have been embarrassed by his mother's pregnancy, but he wouldn't let the baby suffer for it.

"You smell," Finn commented dryly when the baby only stared up at him with wide eyes that matched his own. "I guess I have to clean you."

It was a filthy process, one he hoped he never had to do again. By the time he was done clumsily changing the baby's diaper and cleaning up the resulting mess, Finn was exhausted and wondering why anyone would willingly want to have a baby if it meant doing this every single day. But he pushed on, carefully reading the formula instructions and preparing a small bottle. Not knowing how to hold a baby, he opted for an awkward feeding in the crib, reaching over the bars and pretending not to feel the wood digging into his chest.

"Eat up, baby."

He frowned at his own words. Finn wasn't entirely sure what the baby's real name was. He'd never heard his mother say what she wanted to name him, instead choosing to pretend like her child didn't exist until she absolutely had to acknowledge him. Her attitude didn't surprise Finn—he was used to being ignored, so why would his little brother be any different?

"You need a name. And since I don't know your real name, you can have a code name like me. Makes life more fun that way. I'm Finn, so you can be … Tom!" The perfect match, he agreed with himself. "Finn and Tom. Or Tommy. Or … how about Tom-Tom? I like Tom-Tom."

His little brother so named, he resumed the feeding, hoping he was doing it right. "Slow down," he laughed when some of the formula dribbled from the bottle and down Tommy's chin. With a smile, Finn wiped it away, then gently removed the bottle when the baby was done. Setting it on the bed, he picked up a small figurine and stood it up on the crib railing so the baby could see what he was holding.

"Check this out, Tom-Tom. Made it just for you. I'll keep it on the dresser 'til you're old enough to play with it."

The baby's lively blue eyes stared up at the little boy in Finn's hands. He'd carved it from wood, then wrapped aluminum foil around it like a blanket. Though he knew his brother didn't understand, Finn liked to imagine Tommy knew, in some way, this was a special gift. And when Tommy took hold of the thumb his older brother offered, tiny fingers grasping for contact, Finn felt his heart clench.

Snow had once said he would be a good big brother. How she could know such a thing, he had no idea, but he wanted to prove her right. Sure, she had said it just to be nice, to make him feel good about himself after he'd given her a compliment, but he needed her words to be true. He wanted Tommy to have everything in the world, everything Finn never had, and for the baby to grow up to be happy.

So, yes, he would continue to do this job. He would make Charlie's deliveries, no matter how illegal or scary or dangerous, and he would make sure Tommy never wanted for anything.

CHAPTER 8

THE MUSTANG BANKED a hard left, tires squealing as they searched for traction on the rain-dampened road. From inside the sleek red car, bass thumped against the glass. Finn sat behind the wheel, one hand on the gearshift, the other gripping the steering wheel as he upshifted and raced down the empty side road that would take him to his next delivery.

He didn't worry about speeding. He didn't bother looking around for cops. He wasn't concerned by the fact that he was only fifteen years old, driving with nothing but a permit in his back pocket. None of that mattered, because this was Charlie's car. He was Charlie's kid. Charlie had every cop in the area turning a blind eye.

He was untouchable.

The last two-and-a-half years had been kind to Finn, in more ways than one. He'd worked hard to maintain his bad-ass appearance, putting his body through weekly exercise to build muscle, trying out different hairstyles in the privacy of his own room to see which one made him look toughest, paying attention to what Charlie's men wore to mimic their clothing.

But, more than what he looked like, Finn was determined to learn everything he could about his new world. He'd figured out the rules of the trade early in order to make the money he needed to one day get the hell out of Dodge. Charlie'd even set him up with his own bank account that no one could touch except Finn, least of all his drug-addict mother who'd do anything—and anyone—for a little extra cash. Most of his money went in the bank; the rest was spent making sure Tommy had enough to eat, and medicine from the doctor whenever he needed it. Finn had lost count of the number of times he'd refilled his little brother's nebulizer treatment prescription, or had to get more food because his mother took it all for herself and her latest fling.

A few more years. That's what he kept telling himself. A few more years and he'd be eighteen, and he'd be old enough to get a place of his own away from this hellhole, maybe bring Tommy with him. Make something of himself, even if that meant following in Charlie's footsteps. The man had become a father to him, albeit one who would shoot him in the back of the head if it came down to it. But Finn trusted him, was grateful for the chance he gave a hungry thirteen-year-old kid looking for a job.

He was thinking about the day he first walked into Infinity when he waltzed in the back door, heading straight for Charlie's office. Chix, the bouncer who'd guarded the club for as long as anyone could remember, offered a single nod as he passed by before resuming his typical arms crossed, eyes narrowed pose. Though it was early, the club out front was already packed—a benefit of Infinity being one of the only places in town with cheap alcohol, good music, and a firm "don't ask, don't tell" stance.

Caught up in the music as much as he did the glimpses of scantily clad women, Finn collided with a figure exiting the women's bathroom. "Whoa," he said with a laugh, reaching out an arm to steady the girl, then turning his grin into a playful smirk when he saw who he was holding. "Well, well. We meet again."

The girl, the most beautiful one he'd ever seen, smirked right back. "What's up, loverboy? Got another pickup line for me?"

Not to be deterred, Finn edged a step closer, then another, until her back was against the wall and he had one hand pressed up behind her. She let him drift a hand up her arm, amused, enjoying his efforts. They'd been playing this game for a while—a game she continued to win.

"So," Finn began, ducking his head toward her, "when you gonna agree to that date?"

The sound of her laugh was better than any music Infinity could ever offer, even if it was directed at him. "When you gonna give that up? You know I'm too old for you."

"Only by a year. Doesn't count," he argued back. They'd had this discussion many times. And, just like every conversation in the past, he wasn't going to let his age determine their date. The only thing separating them was her ability to get her driver's license.

In so many other ways, their lives intersected and mirrored. Her father was a known heroin addict, his mother to anything she could get her hands on. Both bought their supply from Charlie. On that, they could commiserate, and often did. Finn had grown up with the girl with jet-black hair, his childhood filled with memories of basketball games and snowball fights and late nights keeping each other company in the cemetery garden when things got too loud and rough at home.

And yet, despite their connection, she still refused him their date.

"I have to go." The hand pressed against his chest lulled Finn out of his thoughts. "Dad's waiting. You know how it is."

She slid out from beneath his arm, offering a wave. But he wasn't done with her yet. "Remember when we used to build snowmen?" he called after her, waiting until she turned to continue. "How cold you used to get? And I was always there to warm you up."

"Yeah," she scoffed back, her expression as bemused as it was saucy, "because you were the one shoving snow down my back."

Seeing his opportunity, Finn followed her down the hall. "Don't act like you didn't enjoy it. So … how about that date?"

She crossed her arms and asked, "Give me one good reason why I should say yes."

Dozens of replies came to mind. Some dirty suggestions he'd heard guys around the club say, some genuine thoughts, some completely bullshit reasons he hoped she'd fall for.

Just tell her how pretty you think she is. Jeez, Finn. It's not that hard. Quit with the dirty stuff and just be honest.

Snow's voice popped into his head. Finn waited, but

she didn't add anything else. What could it hurt, he figured, and replied honestly, "Because I think you're the most beautiful girl in the world, and all I want is one date to prove it to you."

The confession surprised him as much as it did her. Just as it surprised Finn when she smiled and even blushed a little. "Fine. *One* date, loverboy. Meet me at Nero's Pizza at eight."

"I'll be there," he said smoothly, waiting until she had disappeared around the corner to blow out a relieved breath. *Thanks, Snow*, he added, feeling her acceptance of his gratitude as a gloating punch to his gut.

Grinning to himself, Finn got back to business and resumed his trek to Charlie's office. They were waiting for him when he stepped inside.

"About time you showed up," Joe said from the desk, where he was sorting and counting money.

"Bite me," Finn replied. He dropped his backpack next to a table set up in the corner, where one of Charlie's assistants was preparing the evening's deliveries. "Got caught up."

"With Leo's daughter, we heard."

Ignoring Charlie's second hand, Finn headed over to his boss, who was looking down at the club's bar and dance floor through the two-way mirror lining one entire wall. He'd never once seen the older man out there, even when the club was closed to do any inspections or meetings.

"Girls are looking good tonight," Finn commented as he came up beside him. "None as good as my girl though."

Charlie spared him a look out of the corner of his eye. "Your girl is the daughter of one of my clients. If your intentions are anything less than honorable, I would advise you to end your pursuits. We do not mix business with pleasure. You know this."

"Relax, I got this," Finn said before he could catch himself. The glare Charlie directed at him was cold, cold enough to have the boy's insides twisting. "I mean … I really like her, Charlie. I don't have *dishonorable* intentions." When the glare turned to amused pride, he lifted his chin. "That's right. I know some big words."

"So you do." Charlie turned away from the window. "See that your romantic pursuits don't interfere with your work."

"Right, about that." Following his boss to the desk, Finn prepared himself for his next request. He came to a stop across from where Joe sat. Thousands of dollars were spread across the smooth wood, though by now the sight was so commonplace, the teenager didn't bat an eye. "I was thinking, maybe you could give me some bigger jobs. I mean, the runs are good and all and I appreciate the money, but I think I'm ready for more."

Taking a seat next to Joe and reading over a spreadsheet, Charlie didn't look at him as he replied, "More? What kind of more?"

"Well, like this kind of stuff." One hand extended, gesturing to the money. It was a big job to be trusted with the club's cash flow, one typically reserved for a select two or three. As expected, Charlie's brow rose and his expression told Finn there wasn't a chance in hell of that happening. "Okay, so maybe not *this* stuff. But you know what I mean. Something bigger. More responsibility."

Bundling a wad of hundreds, Joe scoffed. "You're a kid. You can't handle more responsibility."

"Yes, I can."

"What, in between math class and recess?"

"Joe," Charlie cut in before a fight could begin. To Finn he ordered, "Go. You have deliveries to make. And, maybe next year when you officially can drive more than the streets here in town, we can talk about this *more* you want to do."

Knowing better than to protest, Finn bit back a sigh and retrieved his bag from the woman in the corner. She had packed it quickly while he spoke to Charlie, and handed it over with a quick nod of acknowledgement.

The bag secured on one shoulder, Finn left the office, not sure if he should feel hopeful or disappointed. He was tired of these runs and wanted to take on the bigger jobs now, but supposed he understood why he had to wait. Technically he shouldn't even be allowed to drive, and only Charlie's influence in town kept him on the road. Bigger jobs meant cops in other cities, where the pull didn't go quite as far.

"Fine, I'll wait," he muttered, taking his keys from his pocket.

A hand gripped his shoulder, breaking Finn from his path to the Mustang. His back hit the wall before he saw who had approached. "What the fuck? What's your problem?"

Joe stood in front of him, fingers digging in his shoulder painfully. "You're my problem, punk," he replied, his voice dangerously low. His hold loosened, only to have his forearm shoved against Finn's chest. "Let's get one thing straight. You're just the help. You ain't one of us."

Never one to back down, Finn set his jaw, eyes narrowed. "I bet Charlie would beg to differ."

"You go runnin' to Charlie and see what happens." They both knew the end result would be one of them bloody and on the floor—and that person wouldn't be Finn. "I'm tellin' you this now, so you listen good. You ain't takin' my place."

Even against the hard arm digging into his collarbone, Finn couldn't help but grin. "What's the matter, Joe? Feeling a little threatened?" As he knew it would, his suggestion had the other man snarling. He expected more, an attempted punch or kick, and was surprised when he was released.

"Watch your back. We both know what happens to people who get in my way." The threat delivered, Joe turned and stalked away, leaving the teenager staring after him, speechless.

After a moment, Finn adjusted his shirt and left Infinity. Yes, he knew what happened to people who got in Joe's way all too well. But he wasn't going to let some asshole like Joe push him around. Finn had goals in life. And putting Joe in his place some day was one of them.

The sun had long set over the horizon when Finn came to a stop outside a bright-green trailer. He had to make this quick, in and out and back to the club. Even though he hated it, he had to study for a test on Monday and prove to Charlie he'd been completing his schoolwork over the weekend. School was Charlie's one condition for working with him. No school, no job. No diploma, no more money.

"*You quit, you get kicked out on your ass. I don't need deadbeats working for me, ya hear?*" He could still hear Charlie's voice in his head the day he'd tried to convince the man to let him drop out.

Shaking his head at his memory of a cocky kid and a boss who couldn't be fooled, Finn jogged up the three steps and rapped on the door, tossing his hair out of his eyes. The sandy-blond locks had gotten long over the past six month, falling around his face in a way the women at the club said would have all eyes on him in a couple years.

Like they aren't already, he thought with an arrogant smirk. He was self-assured enough to know that his looks could easily be his meal ticket if he wanted them to be, all sharp angles and tan skin and panty-dropping grin, and he worked out enough to give his growing body the muscle it needed to look tough. Coupled with his leather jacket and boots, his body and looks were all he had to pride himself in.

He sure as hell didn't take pride in his work, even if he did enjoy a few of the perks.

"You're here! About damn time." Annette Stone, one of Charlie's most frequent customers, answered the door with an annoyed frown. She wrapped a robe around herself as she stepped into the doorway, though not before Finn caught a little flash of skin he knew was on purpose. "How much?"

"Same price as always," Finn answered dryly. "Three hundred even."

The woman sighed, tucking stringy and dull hair behind her ears. She had more wrinkles around her eyes than last time he'd made a delivery, he noticed, and had lost five pounds or so. He wondered how much time she had left.

"I … I ain't got three hundred. Got my shifts cut back at the store." Those wrinkled eyes turned up to Finn, who towered over her a good six inches. Annette offered a pouty smirk, her hands dropping from the edges of her robe to reveal bare breasts and the edges of a lacy black thong. "Maybe we can work out a deal?"

Disgust churned in his gut. It wasn't the first time one of Charlie's clients propositioned him in exchange for drugs—never mind the fact that he was underage—though he'd be lying if he said he didn't enjoy the attention, or the view, from time to time. With Annette, though, he just felt sorry for the woman. "I'm not here to make a deal."

"You sure, honey?" Her fingers grazed her breast, just as she wetted her lips with her tongue.

The revulsion grew until he was snarling at her. "Really? This is how low you've let yourself sink? Just give me the money. You know the rules. Debts have to be paid, not bartered."

Sucking in a sharp breath, Annette took a step back, clearly unnerved by his demand. But she recovered quickly and stomped away with a frustrated huff, returning a moment later with a wad of cash. She all but threw it at his chest, then grabbed the package in his hands. "Get out."

Satisfied, and all too happy to do just that, Finn started to turn, stopping at the bottom of the stairs when she called out to him.

"My parents still talk about you, you know." Finn turned slowly, confused. Annette was still in the doorway as she opened the package. "They meet this bratty little kid for ten minutes and suddenly they want to play hero. Sure as hell never tried to save me, their own goddamn daughter. The hell kinda charm you got?"

"Huh?" The response was a lie. He remembered her parents, the older couple lost in the trailer park while searching for their daughter's home. He also remembered their request, to call them if he ever needed help. "Why would your parents care about me anyway?"

Annette shrugged, taking a quick hit. "Who knows. Couldn't save me, maybe they figure they can save someone in this godforsaken town. Might as well be you."

"Yeah, okay, Annette. See you next week." Brushing off any thought of being saved, Finn jogged back to the car and peeled out of the driveway, eager to get home, knock out a couple hours of studying, then get ready for his date with a certain black-haired beauty who finally agreed to grab dinner with him that evening.

The drive back to the main road was quiet. Too quiet, unnerving even. Finn had learned to suppress Snow's presence when he was on runs or discussing business at the club. He'd made the mistake of letting down his guard in the past, getting caught in the act during one of the rare times he'd taken up one of Charlie's younger clients when she offered to "make a deal." He wasn't eager to relive that lecture.

"Have some respect for yourself," she'd chided over and over again to the sound of his sighs. *"If you can't respect yourself, then at least respect her. You think she likes being that way? You're just helping her hate herself."*

"Got it, Mom," he'd replied before shutting her out.

But he couldn't suppress her for long without feeling empty inside. Finn had come to depend on her voice in his head, and part of him hoped she needed him as much as he needed her. There were plenty of other girls in his life, real girls he'd actually met in person, even one special girl he'd liked since he was a kid. But none of them were Snow. Good, perfect, happy Snow. If she ever decided to leave him, to end this strange friendship built upon fake names and thought-based conversation, he didn't know what he'd do.

He was lost in that thought when a flash of brown darted out in front of him.

"Shit!" he cursed as he swerved to avoid the deer. The Mustang fishtailed on the wet road, the front end missing the deer but the back end swinging into a tree. He heard the crunch of metal even over the bass. It was the sound of pure dread as all feelings of being untouchable vanished thinking about what Charlie would do to him for wrecking his car.

For a moment Finn merely sat in the car, music drowning out his unease, until finally he killed the engine and made his way to the back of the Mustang. "Damnit," he muttered when he saw the smashed taillight, scratched metal, and dented bumper. "Of course you're just fine," he said to the tree.

Letting out a groan of frustration, Finn leaned over the car, resting his head on his arms as he thought about what to do. Pay for the damages, of course. Certainly Charlie wouldn't be pissed over something that wasn't his fault. It wasn't like he was speeding or drinking or any-thing. Just a damn deer.

Yeah, right, he told himself. *Charlie'd kill you over a scratch. This is gonna be a massacre.*

What's up, Finn-Monster? You feel scared.

Finn lifted his head at Snow's voice in his mind, in-stantly feeling a little calmer. *I'm never scared, Snow-*

Glow, he replied, shaking his head at himself and the ridiculous nicknames they'd come up with during one night of rare silly conversation. *Just a little car accident.*

She was quiet for a moment, then asked, *Was it a ... FINNder-bender?*

Despite himself, Finn snorted, then started to laugh, nearly falling over the car as he let himself get lost in the absurd question. It felt good to laugh, something he never really did in a life surrounded by thugs and addicts. He could hear her giggling in his mind, and the thought of her trying hard to laugh in her head so he could hear just made it even funnier.

How long you been waiting to use that one?

Like six whole months.

You are so lame.

Yeah? she challenged. *Well* this *lame girl is at the movies. With a boy. So there.*

He stiffened at that. Even though he didn't have romantic feelings toward the strange girl in his head whom he'd never met—hell, he didn't even know what she looked like, so it wasn't even possible for him to be attracted to her—Finn still felt protective over her. A big brother of sorts, one who would always look out for sweet, innocent Snow-Glow.

"Well then," he said to himself as he got back in the car, ready to face Charlie. "We'll just see about that."

Your parents let you go on a date?

Snow smiled at Finn's incredulous tone. *Yes*, she answered, deciding to leave out the little fact that she was also with six other teenagers. It was a date, as far as she was concerned, since he'd asked *her* to go with him, not their friends.

You're there all by yourself with some guy?

Snow hesitated before replying, *Is that so hard to believe?* It was a cop-out answer and she knew it. But, she figured, she always had to hear about Finn's adventures driving, getting into trouble, going out with girls, doing things she could never do. This one time, she'd make herself sound like fun too.

No way you're there by yourself.

Knowing she was caught, and unable to lie to her best friend, Snow allowed one slip of the truth. *My sister Amelia is here with a date too.*

Yeah? Is she hot?

Finn! Snow shook her head slightly. *She's my sister! Besides, she's too old for you.*

She's like six months older than you and we're the same age. Maybe I should come over, sweep your sister off her feet and make sure your date isn't too lame. Of course, you'd have to tell me where you live for that to happen. And your real name.

Snow rolled her eyes, not surprised by the not-so-subtle reminder that she refused to give up such personal information. He'd been slipping those jabs in more and more lately but still she refused to budge. Thankfully Finn changed the subject before she had to think up a good retort.

What's his name?

Hank.

Hank? She knew by his tone he would follow the question up with something snarky. *What kind of a name is*

Hank? Is he like fifty and balding?

Snow huffed and glanced over at the boy who sat next to her. His green eyes were trained on the movie screen, some kind of action flick. He was cute, in a boy band sort of way, with his gelled hair and Ken-doll face and expensive clothes. Just the kind of boy her parents would approve of, even if she *was* only allowed to go on dates with other friends around.

He's cute, she finally defended her date, smiling at him when he sensed her staring and glanced over. She hoped he wouldn't freak out by her attention being so intently on him, and that he wouldn't notice she was trying to talk to someone in her mind. *He has green eyes and brown hair, and a really great smile. He's in my grade and is a golf player at school.*

Golf, Finn scoffed. *Play a real sport.*

Shut up. He's an awesome player and if he keeps playing this well he might even get a scholarship.

Well color me impressed.

You're just jealous because you are terrible at all sports.

He make a move on you?

Frowning at the sudden change of topic, Snow moved her gaze to the screen, not really seeing the movie as she concentrated on the hand touching her own. *Yes. We're holding hands.*

Wow. Sexy.

Shut up, she said again, and did her best to block him out the rest of the movie. By the time it was over she had no idea what they'd just watched, as she'd focused all her attention on drowning out Finn's constant line of questioning about everything from his grades at school to whether he was a cat or dog person.

Exiting the theater, Snow found herself in the back of the group with Hank at her side. Her friends were busy with talk of the movie mixed with school gossip, leaving her free to speak with her date in private as they entered the humid night air. They had a short walk to the diner next door for milkshakes, then their parents were picking them up.

"I'm glad you came with me tonight," Hank said, squeezing her hand. "Thanks for saying yes."

"Thank you for asking me." Snow smiled sweetly, her grin faltering slightly when he stopped them on the sidewalk, the rest of their friends heading inside the diner. Butterflies swam in her stomach.

I know that feeling. You think he's gonna kiss you.

Be quiet, Snow ordered Finn, annoyed that she'd let her defenses slip. *Maybe I want him to.*

You don't want Hank the Golfer to be your first kiss. He'll probably try to lick you, all up and down your face like a dog.

"Are you okay?" Hank asked.

Snow realized she'd been making a face in response to Finn's comment. "I'm fine. Just got distracted for a second. What were you saying?"

Hank shuffled his feet, looking suddenly nervous. "Just that I think you look really pretty tonight, and … and I was wondering…"

Yes.

Yes what, weirdo?

Crap. "Yes," Snow said aloud, knowing what the nervous teenage boy in front of her was asking. She nearly jumped for joy when Hank moved closer, then closed her eyes when his lips touched hers. It was a gentle kiss, almost chaste, but one she felt in all her nerve endings.

You're kissing the prep, aren't you?

Is it like kissing a fish?

You're not doing a weird stiff-lip thing, are you?

Hey, Snow-Glow. Stop ignoring me.

So did he slip you the tongue?

Stifling a choked gasp, Snow pulled back, ending the kiss. Her first kiss. She smiled at Hank when he took her hand, not seeming to notice what had distracted her.

So, how was the tongue? Did it make you want the—

Finn! Snow cried in her head, a blush tinting her cheeks. *Don't say things like that.*

Prude.

Pig.

They laughed at one another silently. Snow followed Hank inside the diner, and gave him her full attention for the rest of the night.

CHAPTER 9

SOFT LIGHT RADIATED in an oval mirror, reflecting the face of a girl ready to take on the world. Snow stared at herself in the mirror, turning her head this way and that, making sure her hair and makeup were perfect. Golden curls touched her shoulders, complementing the blues of her dress. Her eyes sparkled, lightly dusted in shades of beige and smudged with just enough eyeliner to look intriguing.

It was important she look pretty tonight. Not sexy, but pretty. After all, it wasn't every night she went out to eat with hers and her boyfriend's parents at one of the nicest restaurants in town. Though she'd met Hank's folks many times, they'd never invited her or her family to join them for a meal, so she had to impress them if she wanted to be asked again.

"Good as it's gonna get," Snow said to her reflection, excited for what the night would entail. Lavish night out with both sets of parents, then popcorn and a movie just with Hank in his decked-out entertainment room.

"Are you ready?" her mother called up the stairs. "We need to leave in a few minutes."

"I'm coming!" she shouted back, annoyed at being rushed. "Just a couple minutes!"

Pursing her lips, Snow quickly applied a coat of shiny gloss, already imagining Hank kissing her. He'd kissed her a lot since their first date at the movies two years ago. They'd never gone any further than that, though she knew he wanted to, and liked him even more knowing he was so patient with her when she wanted to wait.

But she was seventeen now. While she still wasn't ready to go all the way, she was thinking she might be willing to do a *little* more than just kiss. Maybe tonight, when they were alone watching the movie, she'd let his hands wander a little more than usual.

Heat rushed through her, the feeling so strange—and so pleasant—that Snow dropped the tube of lip gloss. It clattered to the vanity as her hands gripped the edges, knees suddenly weak. She knew what this sensation was, recognized it from one of the few times she'd gathered up the courage to explore her own body, but this time it was different.

This time, it wasn't her own arousal she was feeling.

"You've *got* to be kidding me," she muttered, desperately trying to sever the connection to Finn, yet some part of her longing to hold on. She'd never felt it like this, so strong and unbridled, so ready to be unleashed. Bottom lip caught between her teeth, Snow found herself closing her eyes and giving in to his subconscious, breath shortening, grip tightening on the vanity.

Finn, she whispered, hating how breathy her voice sounded even in her head, *whatever you're doing ... you have to break the connection. I can feel it.*

Snow? His response was a question and a laugh all at once. *You enjoying the ride?*

Shut up. It just happened.

What did? Ain't nothing happening here ... yet. This is just the previews, baby. Getting ready for the show.

She knew what that meant, how Finn felt in the moments leading up to another bout with a woman. But in the past she'd only felt brief moments of excitement, never this close, and she'd always been able to cut out of the moment. If the *previews* were what she was tuned into, she couldn't imagine how this incredible sensation rushing through her would feel in the throes of passion.

Well just stop until I can break it, then. I have a date and can't go feeling like this.

Feeling like what? You getting sick? Maybe a little feverish? Got the chills? But they both knew the answer. He was messing with her now.

"Time to go!" Her mother's voice startled Snow out of the moment—though not out of her emotions. "You coming or what?"

Despite herself, Snow giggled, torn between embarrassed and aroused. *Mom just asked if I was coming or what.*

So you do know some naughty stuff. He sounded almost proud of her as he laughed. *Now I want to know if you know the feel of a—*

Finn! Red colored her cheeks over the blush she'd just applied. *Don't you have any manners at all! And Hank is waiting for me so stop it!*

Don't mind me, Snow-Glow. Amusement dripped in his reply. *But if you're gonna listen in during your date, at least keep quiet. Maybe you'll even learn a thing or two.*

———

A wry grin crossed Finn's face as he followed the mini-skirted girl currently holding his hand to the back of the club. Music pumped from the main floor, sending deep echoes of bass beneath their feet as they made their way to Charlie's office. His boss would put a bullet in him if he ever found out what his teenage apprentice was about to do, but then again, Finn really didn't give a shit.

He'd been after this girl for years. It had taken him until he was fifteen to even get a date, and now, two years later, she was finally giving him everything else after one hell of a makeout session in his car. That tight eighteen-year-old body, that incredible mouth, even the delicate giggle she reserved only for moments she let her guard down. Not even Snow's earlier intrusion—amusing as it had been—could break him out of this moment.

He locked the door behind them, his hand not even leaving the doorknob before she was tugging at his shirt, lifting it over his head and running her warm fingers over tight abs. He obliged, tossing his jacket and shirt to the floor before grabbing her by the back of the neck and drawing her to him, capturing her mouth with his own. She tasted as sweet as she looked — even if he knew this girl was anything but sweet.

Before he could move lower, she pressed a hand to his chest and pushed him back a few inches. "Not so fast, loverboy."

Finn opened his mouth to protest, only to close it again around her fingers when she held out a pill, prolonging the gesture as a preview of what she was soon to enjoy. She let out a quiet moan that had his insides stirring, then popped a pill of her own and lifted up to her toes.

"You're in for a real treat now," she whispered against his lips.

"Just you wait," he whispered back, surprised by her offering but also thrilled. They both came from junkie parents and typically turned their noses up at narcotics, but in this moment, he was perfectly willing to indulge in a little taste if it meant enhancing the moment with her.

Already Finn felt the effects, his head swimming, the reds and oranges of the office swirling into a kaleidoscope of lust and heat. He saw only black hair and pale skin, emerald eyes staring deep into his own. He felt only her body against his, so soft and supple to all hard parts of him. Their breath left them in gasps as they stumbled back, Finn bracing himself above her as he pushed her up on the smooth oak desk. Skirt hiked up to her hip, legs wrapped around him—his girl was the perfect specimen.

His lips moved to her throat, tasting the soft flesh there, his hands working their way up her arms to her breasts. He reveled in the feel of them cupped so fully in his hands. At the same time, her fingers worked at his jeans, slipping inside the zipper and gripping him, stroking, enough to drive him insane as he floated on the high.

"I want your mouth on me, now," she ordered, looking up at him with those striking green eyes that contrasted her creamy skin and pouty, naturally full lips.

"As you wish," he growled back, all but ripping her shirt away from her body. The rest of her clothes followed until she was naked in front of him, sprawled before his eyes on top of Charlie's desk.

Fuck, this chick is gorgeous, he thought as heated eyes scanned her up and down. His own body tightened in response to the vision before him, urging his hands to work faster as they removed his belt.

"Like what you see?" she purred, fingers dipping beneath her naval, slowly working over her thighs.

He tried, but couldn't speak. Words didn't matter anyway. All that mattered was his mouth on hers, their tongues a dance of want and need; their bodies pressed together, thin sheens of sweat coating them; the sound of their gasps, matching the beat of the bass; his hands on her body, tugging her down by the hips and flipping her so her ass was against him and he was fully primed to go.

Damn, that ass, he said to himself as he appreciated the view before him, fingers working her into a fit of moans. *I can't wait to—*

Gross, Finn!

Snow's voice snapped him out of the moment, startling Finn enough that he stumbled back a step.

I really don't want to hear this!

Then get the hell out of my head! he snapped back, shaking his head to himself as he took his position behind the girl and stroked a hand down her back, slipping lower again, feeling her wet and ready for him as her legs spread.

But Snow wasn't done yet. *You are seventeen years old! Quit acting like some forty-year-old porn star wanna-be!*

Bite me, Snow. And get back to your date so I can get on mine.

Is she at least pretty?

There were so many retorts at the tip of his tongue, but none he could speak as the rolling sensation took him over, inviting him in deeper.

"What the hell are you waiting for?"

Finn blinked, surprised to realize he'd apparently just been standing there staring at her. He quickly composed himself, reaching out and caressing her, enjoying the way her expression changed from annoyance to ecstasy.

She's absolutely fucking gorgeous, he said to Snow, while at the same time replying, "Just getting you nice and ready."

Well, there's that, at least. Have fun.

He could almost feel her leaving his head, a palpable snap of a mutual bond. When he was sure he was alone with his thoughts once more, he gave his girl a seductive smirk that had her biting her bottom lip. That was all the motive he needed to give in to the trip, thrusting them both back into their lust-fueled haze.

CHAPTER 10

LATER, THEY LAY sprawled on the plush rug in front of the desk, still enjoying the effects of their sex-induced high. Out of breath, Finn stared up at the white-plaster ceiling, eyes tracing the swirls of paint in pattern with his fingers gliding over his girl's bare back. Her leg was thrown over his, her warm body pressed against his side.

His thoughts turned to Snow. Good, pure Snow, who would never let a man take her into a dark office with just one goal in mind, would never swallow a pill that would send her into oblivion. He admired her self-control in all things, even if he didn't understand it, and longed for her sense of calmness that always seeped into his mind whenever he needed a break from the chaos of his life. In some strange, twisted way, his unexplainable connection with Snow was his true drug of choice.

"Earth to loverboy," came a sultry voice at his side.

Finn stirred, blinking out of his haze to find emerald eyes staring down at him. "You better be thinking that hard about me."

A mischievous grin crossed his face. "Just remembering you bent over that desk."

"Classy," she laughed while shoving his shoulder, before resting her head in its crook.

Finn enjoyed the way she molded to him, as though she were made to fit him and only him. For a while he concentrated on memorizing her curves, the sound of her breath. The sentimental part of him hoped she would never forget him or this moment. It dawned on him then that he could, just maybe, make sure that didn't happen.

His jacket lay in a crumpled heap next to him. Finn reached over and fished through the pockets until his fingers touched cool steel. "Here."

The dark-haired vision at his side looked up at the object Finn held. It was a person, with a thin body of wire wrapped around wood, legs of twisted paperclips, and an oddly adorable head with tiny stone eyes. A giggle escaped when he made the figure walk up the arm she had draped across his chest, over her shoulder, and plant a kiss on her chin.

"What is this?" she asked, taking the figure from him. "Did you make this?"

"I was bored." He said it nonchalantly, not wanting her to truly understand the meaning of his childhood hobby.

She lifted herself so she was staring down at him. In one hand she held the figure, tiptoeing it along the muscles lining his abdomen. "You have an interesting way of getting rid of said boredom. Can I keep him?"

"I made him for you." Finn regretted the words as soon as they were spoken, hating how vulnerable they made him sound. He was considering saying something rude to counteract the sentiment when she suddenly leapt to her feet.

"Come on. Charlie'll kill us if he finds us in here."

She was giving him the out he wanted, and he could have loved her for it. Finn mimicked her move and rose, finding his clothes in the dimly lit office, not realizing he was being watched until he heard, "So, I came by your place the other night and you weren't there. Is there some chick I'm gonna have to kick in the crotch?"

With a roll of his eyes, Finn pulled his shirt over his head. "No one but you, sexy." He tugged her to him, gripping her still-bare ass to make her laugh. "Besides, I don't live there anymore. I only stop by to check on Tommy."

The response silenced her, so much so that Finn glanced up to find her staring at him with an expression mixed with worry and confusion. "What? Why are you looking at me like that?"

"What do you mean, you don't live there anymore?"

"I got my own place."

"When?"

Exasperated, Finn tugged on his jeans and fastened the belt before moving on to his shoes. "I don't tell you everything, babe. It just happened. I needed to get out of there and be on my own."

She continued to stare at him, dark hair falling in messy waves around her face, then seemed to give up on whatever internal argument she was having with herself. "So," she began, sidling up to him, "where is this new place?"

"Not in town."

"Are you being vague on accident or do you just not want to tell me where your new place is?"

Now Finn paused in the act of dressing, leveling a stare over at his girl. She was standing there buck naked, arms crossed over her chest. He relented and said, "Not being vague on accident or on purpose. The new place just isn't in town. I wanted to get farther away."

"Then where is it?"

He shrugged on his jacket. "Silver City."

"Silver City?" she repeated. "Never heard of it."

"'Cause you've never been out of this hellhole. There's more to the world out there than this shit." Before she could finish dressing, Finn pulled her in for a kiss, enjoying the way she formed to him. "Just gotta make some money, then I can bring Tommy, and maybe even move you in. To my room, of course." He winked, getting a laugh out of the gorgeous girl next to him.

"I think you're still high. I stole the good stuff from my dad."

"So did I," he replied with a smirk. Watching her finish getting dressed, Finn decided he was going to do just that—make a home with the only people he actually cared about.

As though sensing his vow, Snow tugged at his mind, a silent and likely unintentional call for comfort. Finn gave in to the call as he left the office hand in hand with the girl who was now his, letting Snow's soothing aura lead him into tomorrow.

Dinner that night was a lively affair, filled with laughter and conversation and happiness flowing among the two families. The restaurant lived up to its posh name, with sapphire linen napkins perfectly matching earth-toned décor, and soft yellow light glowing from opaque sconces. Cushioned chairs were upholstered in soft grays, the walls a textured stone hue, with dark oak trim to bring the décor together.

At a table toward the center of the restaurant dined two families. It had quickly become clear to Snow this wasn't an ordinary meal, but a cause for celebration—the teenagers' acceptance into their respective colleges, and her father's big win at court.

"Another scumbag brought to justice," Hank's father said as he raised his wine glass in a toast. "I'm happy we could be here tonight to show our respect and appreciation."

"And our gratitude," the lovely woman at his side put in. She was dressed elegantly in a fitted black dress complemented by a sparkling diamond necklace. "I wish there were more people like you to fight for what's right. I admire your courage and conviction to justice."

Snow listened halfheartedly. She'd heard many such praises since she came to live with her family. Everyone knew and loved her father. He worked hard to protect the innocent, and while that sometimes put him in danger from those who didn't want the non-innocent brought to justice, his dedication to *right* and *justness* never wavered. Snow was proud of him too, even if his career was the reason why she was so afraid of strangers, and why, even now, she couldn't let down her guard with Finn.

Finn. She spent most of the evening thinking about

him. She'd finally figured out how to turn off the emotions that had been pulsing through her earlier, but that didn't stop her from imagining what he was doing right now. It amazed her, his life and all the things he got away with, how completely carefree he got to be. Right now, he was likely having intimate moments the likes of which she'd never experienced. Meanwhile, she was having a boring family dinner that would end in a movie with her boyfriend, a little kissing, and maybe some groping over the clothes if she wasn't feeling too shy.

Eventually conversation turned away from talk of politics and law, and to what the future held for the youngest at the table. Hank shared his excitement at earning a golf scholarship, spoke animatedly about business classes he looked forward to taking. When attention was focused on Snow, she found herself answering questions as vaguely as possible.

"Maybe something in education or medicine," was her response to what she wanted to study. "Hopefully someone a lot like me," to an inquiry about her future roommate. The truth was, she wasn't really excited about college. She'd be at the same school as her sister, which made the transition easier. Still, Snow was nervous about moving away from home, even if it was less than a day's drive from the dorms to her house.

"Are you disappointed to be going to a different school than most of your friends?"

Snow shrugged. "I don't have all that many friends, so not really."

Hank's mother nodded as though understanding the girl's loneliness. "Well, I hope you and Hank will be able to remain close. You may be going to different schools but

I know you can find a way. You two are so adorable to-gether."

Smiling, Snow allowed Hank to take her hand. Deep down, though, she wasn't so sure they would stay that close once they both moved away for college. They'd grown close since their first date, enjoying many long talks about their futures. She liked him, there was no question about it, but it saddened her to think about having to leave yet another person behind as she grew up.

"I'm sure these two will find a way," her mother suggested with a teasing smile. "After all, what's college without young love?"

"Or just good friends," her father quickly followed. "Let's not get crazy here."

Snow laughed along with the others, though the conversation twinged at her insides and had her feeling just a little wistful. True, she was looking forward to college and everything that came with it, but it was so much change, and she was afraid of how much she would have to lose in order to gain all these new experiences, all these new friends.

She had a friend, a best friend, one who she could only hope would come with her to college. Snow could always hear Finn, a constant quiet chatter in the back of her mind. Over the years she'd become accustomed to the sound of his thinking, a kind of wordless hum that rarely let actual words or phrases escape unless on purpose. Sometimes they let things slip accidentally, the evening's tryst with a girl a prime example, but they were generally good about controlling their thoughts and emotions.

Sometimes Snow wished he wasn't quite so good at controlling himself. She was fascinated by his life and wanted to hear more about it, as much as he would let her know, anyway. She knew he dealt with some less-than-legal things, and was rather popular with the female population, but that didn't bother her. In her mind, he was living the life only seen in movies, and, truth be told, she was a little jealous.

She wondered, at times, if her parents were right when they brought in Miss Jenn all those years ago. Was Finn truly in her head, a figment of her imagination? An outlet of creativity for an overactive mind that wished to experience far-off adventures and mischief, but didn't want to actually experience the consequences of said mischief? That's what Miss Jenn said, anyway. Snow hadn't forgotten those many visits by the child shrink, the words that made her doubt her own sanity.

She hadn't spoken to anyone of Finn since that first visit, but that didn't stop the sessions. For six months she endured Miss Jenn, and now, a few months shy of her eighteenth birthday, she wondered if she needed a few more months before heading off to college. She found herself waiting for Finn's thoughts, excited to see what kind of trouble he'd gotten into, but he'd been quiet since her invasion into his back room interlude. She'd tried connecting with him a few hours after he shut her out, but she sensed reservation in him, as though he were afraid she would see into the deepest parts of him.

I can't lose him, she thought miserably, staring off in the distance as her parents began reminiscing about their days in college. *He's the only real friend I have.*

Don't worry, Snow-Glow. I ain't going anywhere.

CHAPTER 11

I T WAS LATE by the time Snow finally unburied her nose from the textbook she'd been studying all day. She was surprised to see she was one of the last remaining students in the library. It was finals week, and she hadn't been prepared for the amount of stress that came with it.

Her mind raced with facts and figures, scientific names and numbers. All of a sudden, her goal of being a doctor didn't seem like such a good idea anymore. She'd never doubted that she could do it, but all this studying just to get through her core classes was already starting to wear on her.

With a sigh, Snow glanced at her watch, seeing it was nearing 1 AM. She slowly packed her things and slid out of the chair, weary bones dragging her down the stairs and out of the library. She passed a few lone students here and there on her way to the dorms, wondering as she always did when she could finally get a car and avoid these mid-night walks. Her parents often lectured her on safety, and she heeded their warnings, but there was only so much studying a girl could do in a cramped dorm room with a roommate who preferred video games and late-night talk shows over homework.

Muggy air wrapped around her as she stepped outside, clinging to her skin in a sticky breeze. Even at this late hour the bugs were out full force. Snow ignored them as she hurried down the sidewalk, her mind racing with medical terminology and names of different diseases.

This is really boring, Snow.

Snow paused, surprised, then laughed to herself and kept walking, eyes on the sidewalk. *Sorry.*

Not that I don't appreciate the medical education, Finn continued, *but if you're gonna interrupt what's left of my buzz, at least include some dirty talk.*

Rolling her eyes, Snow shoved her hands in her jacket pockets and tried as she always did to picture Finn. It seemed strange to her now that they'd gone so long without revealing such personal details as their names, addresses, and even appearances. And yet, it felt natural as well, as though they were merely conversing with different aspects of their own selves.

The hell you doing out this late anyway? Finn asked. *Finally getting yourself into some trouble of the male persuasion?*

Snow huffed. *Excuse me, I'm a good southern gal bred in the Bible Belt. We never kiss and tell.*

That sounds incredibly dull. Good thing I'm a bad northern boy.

Bad enough for the both of us, she replied, then wondered if he had the same jolt of realization that they'd just shared something revealing a little piece of themselves. At his silence, she quickly asked, *Why are* you *out this late?*

Heading home from a party.

But you said you had a buzz. When Finn didn't answer, Snow frowned. *Finn. It's bad enough you drink underage, but seriously, you're driving too?*

Alone in the Mustang save for the nagging voice in his head, Finn grimaced. The girl really was killing his buzz.

Lay off, Snow, he thought over the beat of the bass. *I ain't that bad off.*

Still, you know better than that, Finn. Be smart.

Her words grated on his last nerve. He'd already had a rough night of out-of-the-way deliveries, his chick nagging him about how he never took her home to his place, and a phone call from Charlie that he couldn't think about just now, not until he got back and figured out what the hell he was going to do. The last thing he needed was Snow mothering him.

He was twenty goddamn years old. He could take care of himself.

Sometimes he resented how sweet Snow was, so innocent and sheltered with parents who adored her and a sister who was always there when she needed her. Snow got to be the nice one, living in her perfect world, never having to worry about a damn thing except what college class to go to and what rich guy to marry after graduation.

He didn't have those luxuries. He didn't always know

where his next meal was coming from, or whether or not he'd be able to get Tommy a new inhaler next month. His home was broken, his family fractured, and these days all he lived for was making sure Tommy had something to eat, and, hell, was at least still alive. Work from Charlie kept his bank account in the green, but Finn was on his own now, had to be an adult. Even if being an adult meant the jobs got more dangerous and he found himself a little deeper in a world that would surely put him down a path that led six feet under.

Angered by his own reflections, Finn searched the passenger side for the bag he'd dropped there before peeling out of his friend's driveway. He knew there was a bottle in there somewhere. He needed a drink, something to take his mind off Charlie's phone call and the reason why he was heading home.

Finn? Maybe you should pull over and call a friend to bring you home so you aren't driving drunk.

The voice in his head interrupted his move to grab the bottle. It was like she knew every goddamn time he was doing something wrong. *Snow, just shut the fuck up, okay?* The words slipped in his mind before he could filter them. He could feel the hurt they caused, but was too worked up, and a little too drunk, to care. *You live your perfect little life in your perfect little college and be a perfect little girl. Some of us have real life to deal with, and real life ain't so pretty.*

It was a good minute before she responded. *Okay ... I'm sorry, Finn. I just ... I just want you to be safe.*

Stop worrying about me. I got a mother, useless as she is. I sure as hell don't need another one.

I'm not trying to be your mother. There was an edge

to her voice now, one he hadn't heard before. *I'm trying to be your friend. You're my best friend whether you like it or not, so you have to put up with me telling you to stop being stupid and grow up already, got it?*

Anger seeped into his thoughts, a cold kind of hate, and for once he didn't care if he let those feelings transfer to Snow. *If that's all you got to say, then you shut the fuck up and—*

Finn, wait.

Don't pull that shit with me. I got something to say and—

Finn, I think I'm in trouble.

He hesitated, hands gripping the steering wheel as he wondered if this was a trick. *What do you mean?*

There's this huge guy coming toward me and he's holding something but I can't tell what it is. He's wearing a mask but I can see his arms. They're covered in tattoos. I don't know what to do.

What? Worry overtook anger in a heartbeat. *Where are you?*

Walking home from the library.

In the middle of the night? He cursed inwardly to himself. *Snow, tell me exactly where you are. No bullshit.*

The campus library, she replied, her words laced with panic. *He's calling to me. He knows my name. Finn, there's another one behind me.*

His breath caught in his throat and the road in front of him tunneled. *Snow, get the fuck out of there. Run. Drop everything and run as fast as you can. Scream for help.*

His heart began to race, hands trembling. With a gasp he realized he was feeling what Snow felt — panicked, out of breath, heart pounding in tune with racing footsteps. He heard her panting breaths in his mind. His foot slammed on the brake, the car sliding to a stop in the middle of the street, the squeal of tires on pavement mixed with pumping bass rising higher than her cries.

Finn! They're chasing me! Finn!

"Snow!" His shout filled the Mustang—a flustered and pointless attempt at help. He stumbled out of the car, needing to get away from the distracting music, needing to hear her, help her. In his head he heard her heavy panting as she ran, in his stomach he felt the nauseating fear.

Run, Snow. As fast as you fucking can. Just run!

Finn! I can't—There're too fast!—Fi—

Her words cut off, ending in a high-pitched scream that drowned out his surroundings. Finn dropped to his knees on the pavement, hands pressed to his temples. *Snow! Snow, talk to me! Where are you! Can you see their faces?*

Finn! He's got a gun!

Where are you! he repeated, desperation shouting across his mind. *Tell me something, Snow! What do they look like!*

Tattoos on his arms! Snow managed between shrieks that were starting to sound more and more muffled. *Skinny guy, dark hair gelled back! Tech—*

Snow screamed, the sound filled with fear and pain and desperation. There were no more words now, only yelps and cries, gasps brought on by painful blows, screeches that brought tears to Finn's eyes as he experienced the attack with her. He felt every punch to the face, every kick to the ribs, his insides churning and clenching and pleading for escape.

In the middle of the road, Finn rocked, the grip on his

head tightening. In some far-off place he realized he was screaming too, a throaty howl that matched the wailing voice consuming his mind, despair overtaking his spirit as he realized he could do nothing but listen as his counterpart was beaten, battered, brutalized.

And then the world went silent.

CHAPTER 12

H E DIDN'T KNOW how long he sat there in the road, rocking on his knees, whispering pleas to himself to hear her voice again. It wasn't until a horn blasted through the early-morning air that he moved, falling back against his car. Whoever had approached wasn't concerned enough to stop and kept driving. Finn was grateful. He wasn't sure he could speak right now, let alone even get up off the road.

She was gone. He could feel her absence like a shovel digging out parts of his soul. The normal dull hum of chatter was gone, replaced by the drone of frogs and crickets that surrounded him. Was she dead? Did those men, whoever they were, did they … He couldn't even think the word, let alone fathom its reality.

"Snow?" Finn whispered, his voice cracking. "Snow, are you there?" He sniffed, realizing hot tears had fallen down his cheeks. Quickly he wiped them away with the sleeve of his leather jacket, then dragged himself into the driver's seat of his Mustang. For a moment he simply sat there, not knowing what to do.

He could go to the police. And tell them what? That a girl he'd talked to in his head since he was seven was attacked? That he didn't know her name, but she lived somewhere in the south and went to college? They'd laugh him out of the station or lock him up in the closest crazy house.

He could go to the college himself, wherever it was. And do what? Walk down every street in every town in every Bible Belt state searching for a huge guy with tattoos on his arms and a skinny guy with dark hair? He'd get nowhere, fast.

He could do some kind of online search for kidnapped women. Or … murdered, he finally thought with a hard swallow. But it just happened. There wouldn't be any news about the attack yet, and even if there was, there wouldn't be enough details to figure out a starting point.

He could…

Finn didn't know. There was nothing he could do except sit in his car and mourn the fact that the last thing he'd ever said to Snow was to shut the fuck up.

The sun was just starting to rise when he finally stumbled home, a bitch of a hangover starting to take hold and his body begging for sleep despite rushing with adrenaline. Finn only stopped long enough to take a drink of water straight from the tap before racing to his room.

Piles of clothes, some dirty, others clean but unfolded, lined the floor, along with discarded pizza boxes and soda cans. Charlie harped on him about being a slob, but Finn could never be bothered to clean. There were more important things to worry about. In this moment, he wished he'd listened, because somewhere under that mess was his laptop.

"Goddamn it," he grumbled as he tossed clothes all over the place. "Where the fuck is it?"

After a few minutes of searching Finn finally found the slim black computer beneath a heap of shirts and all but slung it on the scarred wooden desk. His fingers twisted a rusty paperclip as the old laptop booted up, knee bouncing, eyes a little blurry and head spinning. Part due to alcohol, part at a loss to this foreign feeling of complete nothingness inside him.

He had to find her.

Finally online, Finn prepared to search the web … then paused, fingers hovering over the keyboard, not having any idea where to start. In the thirteen years he'd been talking to Snow, they'd never once said where they lived—him because he was embarrassed of where he came from, her because of some irrational fear of strangers. Now he realized how foolish, how incredibly stupid, they had been.

Why wouldn't you just tell me who you are, Snow?

No response. Not even the hint of her aura. How the hell was he supposed to find her when he couldn't talk to her anymore?

He had only one clue to go on. "Bible Belt. She said she lived in the Bible Belt," he muttered, his mind racing to think of a search that would make sense. "What states is that … shit." Finn sat back with a sigh when his search yielded a map covered by far too much red. She could be anywhere in the southern United States.

"No." Continuing his one-sided conversation, Finn thought back to all the conversations he'd ever had with Snow. There had to be something, *anything*, to narrow it down. "The beach. She went to the beach a lot."

That cut out the landlocked states. "It was the same time there as here."

He did a quick search on time zones, narrowing down his focal point a little more. But there were still so many places to search. The Carolinas, Georgia, Florida, Louisiana ... assuming he was even on the right path. What if she moved away from the beach for college? Was she now in one of those landlocked states he'd just disregarded?

Stuck, Finn shook his head to wake himself up as his mind continued to race, thoughts and ideas fizzling before they could form actual plans. "There's got to be something." Desperate to find even the tiniest bit of information, he typed in *southern states kidnapping college campus* then waited to see what results popped up.

News of several abductions filled the page, all from previous years. "Shit." There was nothing from today. No updates of a young woman kidnapped in the middle of the night on her walk home. "Because they don't even know yet," he said to himself, hands starting to tremble and his eyes drooping in surrender to the defeat filling his heart.

Forcing his body to steady, Finn took in a deep breath and rubbed his eyes, trying hard to focus on the computer, on Snow, on what he could possibly do. It never felt this hard before, thinking and analyzing and coming up with a plan. Snow was always there to help him, if not directly than with the inspiration her presence gave him. Without her, without her spirit filling all the empty parts of him, he couldn't even see a way to take his next breath.

As though his body understood such a despairing thought, Finn slumped over the desk, alcohol, exhaustion, and utter confusion overtaking him. As he drifted into unconsciousness despite the anger and fear pulsing through him, all he could think was that, once again, he had failed Snow.

A heavy pounding behind his eyes woke Finn from a heavy sleep. Grogginess clouded his vision, nausea churning in his gut, as he pushed up from his desk and struggled to remember where he was, how he got home, why it felt like he'd slept hunched over all night.

The pounding came again, and he realized it wasn't just behind his eyes—it was also at the front door. With a garbled curse, Finn pushed up from the desk and stumbled down the hall to the door, wrenching it open.

"What?" He regretted the bitterly spoken word as soon as he saw who was demanding a presence with him. "Oh. Hey, Joe."

The hulking brute of a man crossed his thick arms. "Where've you been? Charlie's demandin' you come in. Get your shit together and let's go. And wash up. You look like shit."

Finn knew better than to argue with Charlie's number two. He may hate the man, but he was still second in charge. "Yeah, okay. Just let me grab my jacket." Turning, he retreated to his room, unable to shake the nagging feeling he was supposed to be doing something much more important as he shrugged on the leather jacket. Sighing against a growing migraine, he nearly left the room when his open laptop caught his eye. The screen was dimmed but clearly showing a live feed of a news station.

Memories of last night slammed into him. Charlie's phone call. Driving home as fast as he possibly could. Snow scolding him, him yelling at her.

Snow screaming, then nothing but silence.

Finn slid into the desk chair, focused entirely on the screen. He turned the volume up, eyes scanning the monitor to see he was on a Georgia news station. The morning news was being played, two anchors sharing details he only caught the tail end of.

"...abducted from campus around approximately one AM last night. Her parents contacted local police when she couldn't be reached this morning, and her roommate confirmed she never arrived home last night. Campus officials reviewed security tapes and discovered this chilling footage."

The nausea in his gut returned as Finn stared at the screen. The footage was dark and grainy, but clearly showed what he feared—a young woman being tracked by two men in black, surrounded, her mouth open in an unheard shout for help, then struck multiple times into unconsciousness. As he watched, Finn heard those silent screams in his head, echoing and echoing until they, too, faded away into mere memory.

The anchors were still talking, but he couldn't hear them over the pounding in his head, the deafening roaring in his ears as his eyes trained on one spot on the screen. Security footage had disappeared, replaced by an image in the upper right-hand corner. A young woman, just a girl, really, with curled blonde hair, lively blue eyes, porcelain skin, and a smile that spoke of kindness and purity.

"Snow. There you are, Snow," he whispered, voice catching on the single word, lips parting in shock as he tried to make sense of what he was seeing. She looked exactly like he'd always imagined, such light and happiness and innocence, an angel to his devil, but it was so much more than that. He was drawn to her, wanted to protect her. Kill for her.

He had to find her.

"The hell you doing?" Joe shouted from the other room. Heavy steps stomped into the bedroom, a strong hand grabbing him by the back of the jacket. "Ain't time for computer browsing, boy. Charlie's looking for you."

Before he could argue, Finn was yanked off his feet and dragged down the hall, all but thrown into Joe's car outside. All the while he struggled to come up with one of many plans, though none of them made sense.

He had to go to Georgia. *You take Charlie's car without permission, he'll kill you.*

He was going to find her. *You don't know where she is.*

He would kill those mother fuckers who hurt his friend. *You barely know what they look like.*

He would save Snow. *You don't even know if she's still alive.*

Searching internally, Finn listened for her voice, tried to feel her presence. Not for the first time, he wondered if he was crazy after all, that Snow had been a voice in his head all along. But just as soon as he thought it, he pushed the notion away. No, he knew Snow was real. She was part of him. Or, she used to be. Now he was drifting amidst a sea of his own doubt and fear. Where she once consumed him, there was nothing.

Just an empty silence he didn't know what to do with.

CHAPTER 13

"WHERE THE HELL have you been?"

Charlie stared up at him from behind his desk, his eyes a terrifying mix of furious and something Finn couldn't quite identify. Worry? Murderous? Whatever it was, years of receiving any kind of glare from the man had taught Finn not to fidget, but to put on as brave a front as possible, even if he didn't really feel it inside.

"I called you last night. You said you were on your way. I want to know what happened."

He nearly told the truth before fear held him back, an uncertainty that he wouldn't be believed. So he chose a lie instead. "I was on my way. Guess I had too much to drink and forgot and went home instead."

Finn tried to take a step back when Charlie rose, but Joe was standing behind him, blocking his escape. "You chose to get drunk instead? You *forgot*?" the older man growled, unusually grouchy compared to his normally calm and collected exterior. "This is unacceptable. I've put up with your shit long enough. If you—"

"I need some time off," Finn cut in before he could talk himself out of the interruption. He set his jaw when Charlie stiffened and crossed his arms.

For a moment, the two engaged in a long stare-off, until the younger boy relented, knowing his place. Charlie nodded when Finn's eyes lowered. "Time off," the man repeated slowly, his voice strangely quiet. "You better have a good reason for saying those two words to me right now."

"I know, I just..." He couldn't tell Charlie the truth. He'd think he was crazy. But, he could at least let his boss know he wasn't just slacking off. "Look, a friend of mine is in trouble, asked me to help her out."

The anger in Charlie's eyes faded slightly, replaced by that same emotion Finn couldn't place earlier. "Her? What kind of trouble we talking about here?"

"I'm not sure," Finn was quick to say, seeing the conversation possibly going his way. "But she asked me for help and I promised to be there. Look, that's all I can say. I need a week to get to Georgia and help her. I've got some money saved to cover the cost. I can—"

"Stop," Charlie commanded, holding out a hand. "I don't have time for this. I have things to take care of at home, which you were made aware of when we spoke last night. You need to be here, and that is final."

Finn hesitated, wanting to fight for himself and for Snow, unsure what would happen should he cross his boss. He steeled his nerves and replied, "I need to be there. And I won't take no for an answer."

The air stilled, deadly in its silence. Finn felt his heart beat harder and his fingers threaten to tremble. But he stood tall, even when Charlie stalked around the desk slowly, a predator after prey, stopping only when he towered over his apprentice.

"Have you forgotten who you're talking to?" Charlie asked in a calm, controlled voice everyone recognized as the tone that preceded a bloodbath. "Do you think I'm a foolish old man who can be bossed around by a child?"

"...No," Finn answered after a beat, trying to think of the right thing to say to keep the man from burying him. "I just ... She's special to me and ... if I don't help her, it might be too late. She needs me. I'm all she's got."

"And who is this precious friend?"

"A girl I've known since I was little. She doesn't live in town." That much was true. "You don't know her."

Charlie's eyes narrowed. "How convenient."

The accusatory tone stiffened Finn's back. "I'm not lying, Charlie. I know better than that. She needs me, and I'm wasting time standing here trying to convince you to let me go."

"You think I'm going to let you run off to God knows where? You've been working for me for many years, but that doesn't mean you can do whatever you want, whenever you want, no matter what personal issues you have. Not in this business."

"Then send someone with me," Finn argued back, determined to win this battle. "I'm not looking to do anything shady, Charlie. I just need some time to take care of my friend. If that means having a babysitter, then fine."

Eyes narrowed, Charlie stared down the young man before him, begrudgingly impressed when Finn didn't flinch or look away. "A babysitter," he muttered, jaw working as he thought it over. "Fine. If this is what you have to do, then so be it. But Joe will be going with you."

Joe, who had said nothing from his place by the door since delivering Finn, straightened, his face a portrait of indignation. "Charlie, I ain't some babysitter for the punk. You can't think he's being serious. Kid's clearly planning somethin' and with everythin' else going on—"

"This is neither a negotiation nor a request," Charlie cut in smoothly, his icy blue eyes never leaving Finn. "You will go, and you will both return in one week. You have until noon to make your preparations, then the clock starts."

"And make no mistake," Charlie continued as Finn turned to leave, ready to race out the door. "When your week is up, you *will* return to this spot, and you *will* tell me exactly what happened."

Offering a single nod, Finn rushed past Joe, heading for his car. He only had a few hours to prepare to save Snow.

NOTHING SHORT OF shock accompanied him on the drive to the trailer park. Finn hadn't expected Charlie to relent, especially that fast and suddenly, agreeing to give him some time away from the club to deal with his "personal issues," as his boss put it. Just as he hadn't expected help along the way, some money for the road. Still, Finn understood the rules.

He was given a week. Seven days to figure his shit out and save Snow. He'd worry about what to tell Charlie when he got back.

"What the hell am I going to do?" he muttered as he pulled into the driveway he hated most. These days he came by once a week, and it was only to check on his younger brother. Tommy was seven now, old enough to know his life was shit and his mother even worse, but not old or strong enough to do anything about it. The sickness that plagued him as a baby and toddler was still ever present in his lungs, making him prone to asthma attacks and harsh coughs that, more than once, led to bronchitis or pneumonia. His ailments only made it that much harder for Finn to leave him behind.

Biting back a sigh, Finn steeled his nerves and ordered himself to keep his cool before exiting the car and all but stomping up the rickety steps. The front door swung open—locks were never one of his mother's few concerns—and the odor of sweat, smoke, and stale alcohol nearly choked him.

Nothing ever fucking changes, he thought bitterly, then followed his thought with an automatic, *Sorry, Snow*.

The silently spoken words froze his feet as sorrow swept through him. Over the years he'd grown so used to apologizing for cursing that it was habitual. Snow hadn't always replied to his random, everyday thoughts, but always was there to remind him to watch his language.

Now she was gone, the person he depended on most merely a name he whispered in his head.

"I'll get you back," he spoke the promise and pushed through the mess of the house, to his old room. At his back, his mother's bedroom door was closed, and he guessed she likely was either passed out with a bottle in her hand or had her head in some guy's lap.

The room was quiet when he entered, light spotted on

the wall through a frayed curtain. On the bed, the same bed Finn had used growing up, was Tommy, still sound asleep. Finn sat on the edge of the bed and bounced a couple times, unable to keep from grinning when his brother muttered a complaint.

"Rise and shine, Tom-Tom. We got places to be."

"Don't wanna," the boy whined, trying to cover himself up with a tattered blanket. "Tired."

Finn chuckled but pulled the blanket off, then grabbed an old backpack from the floor, stuffing whatever clothes he could find that seemed somewhat clean inside. A couple toys were added before he zipped the bag up and clapped his hands once, startling his brother.

"Come on. We gotta go."

"Go where?"

Pulling Tommy up by his shoulders, Finn tossed a set of clothes at him, waiting until the boy begrudgingly began to dress. "I have to go on a trip, and need to make sure you're taken care of while I'm gone. Come on. It'll be fun, I promise."

Not giving his brother time to argue, Finn helped him dress the rest of the way then slung the bag over his shoulder, leading Tommy out of the room, through the sludge of empty bottles and dirty clothes that lined the hallway.

"The hell you think you're going with my stuff?"

The slurred voice slowed him down, but didn't stop his forward trek to the front door. Only when his mother blocked his path did Finn finally look up at her. "Your stuff?" he repeated incredulously. "Your ability to love continues to amaze me."

"Don't act like you're so perfect and innocent," she spat back. One hand braced herself against the couch; the other gripped the neck of a clear glass bottle. Her eyes dropped to the bag at his shoulder. "The hell you doing?"

"Going on a trip. An actual trip, not one you find with a needle."

She scoffed. "Like you ever gave a shit. So you got money now. Doesn't give you the right to barge in here and take what's mine."

He could have reminded her he came every week with food—food she likely ate herself or gave to one of her many boyfriends—or that every piece of clothing Tommy owned was purchased with his own money. He could have thrown the boy's illness in her face, or told her exactly what he thought of her mothering skills. But he knew it would have been on wasted breaths, so instead he merely said, "If you can tell me how old Tommy is, he'll stay."

The set of her jaw and narrowed bloodshot eyes as she stared at him in confusion gave him his answer. Finn pushed his mother out of the way and dragged Tommy by the wrist out the door, to the car, ignoring the string of profanity being shouted at his back.

Only when they were away from the trailer and stopped at a gas station, having loaded up on snacks, did Finn finally let himself breathe. It was now or never.

Retrieving his wallet from his back pocket, Finn thumbed through the few cards and folded-up bills until he found the card he needed. One he'd had for years, never able to throw away, never able to explain why he kept it.

His mother's voice filtered into his head. *We don't ask for help. We are better than that. You got that, you little shit?* Pride battled with common sense, years-old mantras stuck in his head after being beaten into his body.

Memories of those fists, those bitterly spoken words, had him all but punching numbers into the phone.

"Hi," he greeted when a man's voice picked up on the other end. "You probably don't remember me, but I'm calling in that favor now."

TOMMY COMPLAINED THE entire drive. "Why do I have to go to some old person's house? Why can't I stay home?"

"Because I need to make sure someone is actually taking care of you while I'm out of town," Finn replied, though he didn't voice the second part—that while he'd told Charlie he only needed a week, and while that was all his boss had allowed, he was planning on being gone as long as it took, and guessed his search for Snow would take longer than seven days.

"I can take care of myself."

"Oh, really?" Finn spared his brother a sarcastic glance. "What kind of medicine do you take? When do you take it? Are you supposed to eat before you take it?" The boy's silence was rewarded with a sarcastic laugh. "That's what I thought. Besides, you'll like it there."

It felt wrong, a little dirty even, to be entrusting his little brother's care to two virtual strangers. But Finn considered himself a good judge of character—a trait he'd picked up after working with Charlie for so long—and he'd heard many stories of these people straight from the one who knew them best.

Besides, he added to himself, *there is no one else in this shithole state I can trust. Might as well be them.*

His earlier phone call led him to a ritzy neighborhood

far too stuffy and glamorous for his tastes. His black Mustang was out of place against the rows of perfectly manicured boxwoods and flowing green seas of grass, well-maintained streets and long driveways with intricate paver designs.

Speeding through wide-landed streets, Finn finally reached his destination: a narrow road tucked away in the deepest part of the neighborhood away from prying neighbors. At the end of that road, a black metal gate opened for him as he approached. Finn drove through slowly, winding down the long drive to a house that might as well have been a palace for all he knew. Tommy's eyes were wide, his expression filled with awe and envy, though Finn merely shook his head. All these people had was money, didn't make them any better than him.

The man who greeted him at the front door was familiar, one of two faces burned in his memory. He never forgot the old couple who called him off the front stoop of his trailer, showing concern for a child clearly in need of help but too proud and stubborn to ask for it. For a while he told himself he remembered them out of anger—how dare those old people act like he needed them and all their money, he'd think—but as he got older he realized a big part of him wished he'd gone with them all those years ago.

They couldn't save him now, but, maybe, Tommy would have the chance meant for Finn.

Stepping up to the front door, Finn found himself face to face with old man Stone, as so many kids in his neighborhood called him when referencing Annette Stone's father. Others knew him by a name Finn had always found ridiculous—"Top Pop," a moniker that spoke of his prominent standing in town.

No matter his name or his success, Finn saw old man Stone as any other person and spoke to him as he would a business partner. "You said once that if I needed you, you'd be there to help," he said evenly. "Well, it may be a few years too late, but I need that help now, and I need it to be taking care of Tommy until I get back."

Curious and concerned eyes stared back at him. Before the other man could argue, Finn continued, "I know who you are, and I know you know who I am. If you agree to take care of Tommy, then you can't tell anyone you have him. I can't have my mother finding out where he is and doing something stupid like she always does. I don't know is how long I'll be gone, but I promise I'll be back. I won't leave him behind."

For a moment, neither of them spoke. Tommy sat on the front step, already bored by the conversation. Old man Stone remained in the doorway, peering across the threshold at Finn with an odd expression of sadness. "What's going on, son?"

"Nothing I want to concern you with." The *why* wasn't what mattered, and he had neither the time or desire to explain it. "I just need someone to be with Tommy, someone I can trust. I know I don't really know you, but I know of you, and that has to be good enough."

Waiting for a response nearly had Finn lashing out in anger, impatience brimming beneath the surface of his skin. Finally, old man Stone nodded. "My wife and I offered you help when we knew you needed it, but you refused. If helping you now is what you need, then the offer still stands, for as long as you need it. You don't have to worry about Tommy."

"Good. Thank you." It felt awkward, thanking some-one for doing him a kindness.

"...Are you sure there's nothing more you need? Something I should know about?"

Finn pulled out his keys and forced himself not to think about what he was doing, the risk he was taking in leaving his little brother in the hands of a man he'd barely met. "You can take care of Tommy. That's all I need."

Not waiting for a reply, Finn knelt down at the step and nudged his brother, trying to coax a grin out of him. "Hey," he said quietly, waiting until Tommy looked up at him, hesitation and sadness in his big blue eyes. "I made this for you." Finn pulled a palm-sized figure out of his pocket and held it out to his brother. Carved of wood, the little boy was a replica of the seven-year-old, painted with blond hair and a silver shirt etched to look like armor. A tiny sword twisted out of wiring was wrapped around the wooden boy's hand.

"He's a superhero, like you." Finn tried to get Tommy to take the figure; when his offering was refused, he set it down on the step next to his brother. "Take it when you're ready. He'll keep you company until I get back. And I will be back, okay? I promise."

Then he turned on his heel and stalked down the stone steps, wondering if he'd be able to keep his promise.

CHAPTER
14

FINN'S LAST STOP was his apartment. It didn't take him long to pack, although to him it felt like the entire day had passed before he was finally ready to make the long drive to Georgia. In one large duffle bag he packed a few changes of clothes and an extra pair of boots, what little toiletry items he actually owned, and three guns—one a gift from Charlie on his eighteenth birthday, one a weapon he'd taken from a junkie who overdosed right in front of him, and the third one of Joe's rejects that would have otherwise gone to the scrapyard. He wasn't a great shot and didn't have any weaponry skills to boast about, but Finn knew the game. It wasn't always about the shot, but about who fired first.

When he was finally ready, his bag filled with nothing but necessities, he grabbed his keys from the counter and an energy drink from the fridge. It was going to be a long drive. He couldn't risk flying, not with everything he'd packed beneath the messily folded clothes.

Locking the door behind him, Finn turned to jog out to his car, pausing when he saw the man leaning against the hood. "So you're actually coming along, huh?"

Joe pushed himself off the car, arms crossed. With his black shirt stretched across hard muscle decorated with tattoos, dark jeans, and thick boots worn with age, he looked every bit the part of town thug. "Not like I was given a choice in comin' along for the ride."

"Or we could both agree to go our separate ways now and keep it between us. Consider it a vacation." When the man only stared, Finn continued, "What, you don't trust me or something?"

"Or somethin'," Joe replied casually. "We goin' or what?" he asked when Finn just stood there staring at him. Neither moved for a moment, a silent war of wills.

"Get in," Finn finally said on a sigh, knowing this was not a battle he would win. So he would agree and bring Joe along, then ditch him as soon as he could.

"Where we goin', anyway?"

Where, Finn repeated to himself. Wasn't that just the question? To a state he'd never been to, a city he was only guessing at, and a girl he still wasn't convinced actually existed. He must have been out of his goddamn mind.

"Atlanta," he answered. The reply came from nowhere, surprising even him. Until this moment he hadn't actually thought of a destination other than Georgia. Atlanta worked, though. It was a big enough city, well known, and would hopefully serve as a good starting point for his search.

"Atlanta? And we're driving?" Joe shot a grimace over at Finn, then nodded when realization dawned.

"Gotcha, kid. Ain't travelin' with plane-approved cargo."

The man's easy acceptance surprised Finn, though he didn't comment. Instead he glanced down at his phone, angling the screen away from Joe as he scrolled through Georgia news stations, hoping for more updates, but either he couldn't find the right website or there was nothing new to know.

"The hell you doing?" Joe asked, annoyance clear in his tone. "Thought you were in a hurry and here you are dickin' around online."

Frustrated, Finn dropped his phone in his lap and moved to start the car, only to be hit with a wave of nausea that started behind his eyes, racing through his head and hitting his gut like a sucker punch. Instantly he was leaning over the steering wheel, torn between trying not to hurl and hoping, praying, this rushing sensation coursing through him was the return he'd been waiting for.

"Hey—what's wrong? What's goin' on?" At his side, Joe shoved at his shoulder, appearing genuinely concerned for the first time, but Finn could only concentrate on the pulsing of sickness jumbled with relief.

He smelled mustiness and mold, tasted blood, so much so he checked to make sure his mouth wasn't bleeding. And he hurt. Everywhere, he hurt, feeling like he'd had the shit beaten out of him. His head snapped up at the thought, his vision blurring. This was what she felt, how she must be feeling now in the aftermath of the attack.

Snow.

A flickering sensation fluttered in the back of his head. A hint of a weak presence, a thought trying to slip into the forefront of his mind. He tried again. *Snow. Please, Snow, let me know you're still there. Tell me—*

Finn.

It was only one word, one whispered name mixed with tears before his world went silent again, but it was enough. Now he had proof; he knew he was right to start his search. Snow was alive, somewhere, somehow, and he could only imagine what was happening to her as she tried so hard to reach him.

I'm coming, Snow.

Water stains crisscrossed a worn ceiling, the steady dripping a grim lullaby to the girl sleeping fitfully on a dirty bed in the corner of a chilly room. Night air whistled in through a crack in the boarded-up window, slowly waking the young woman, coaxing her bruised and bloodshot eyes to open and take in their new reality.

Her first awareness was pounding. A hard, excruciating pounding deep in her head that made it feel as though her eyes would soon burst from her skull. Snow struggled to sit up, bracing herself with one shaky hand as the other went to her forehead. A wave of nausea swept through her, starting in her stomach and burning its way up to her throat. Her vision swam as she swallowed back the sickness.

Sitting perfectly still, Snow let her consciousness travel from head to toe, taking stock of her injuries and her surroundings. Cold air. Small, boxed-in room. Bed that smelled like death. Skin aching from the inside out. That was as far as she got before her body revolted against her and she vomited over the side of the mattress, tears building and a pathetic whimper escaping dry lips. For a moment all she could focus on was the nausea and pain, before flashes of the beating she'd endured pushed through the agony.

The men. The fists, so many fists, raining down on her body. She'd tried so hard to fight, screaming for help, begging Finn—

Finn.

She felt it then, a presence within her telling her she wasn't alone. Relief flooded through the pain when she heard his promise. *I'm coming, Snow.*

He was coming for her, coming to save her, protect her. But how? She didn't even know where she was. How would Finn ever be able to find her?

With renewed hope lined with fear and doubt, Snow glanced around in hopes of seeing something she could use to identify her location, but there was only a tiny bedroom with smoke-stained yellow walls, dingy gray carpeting, and an old wooden dresser next to what she guessed was a closet. A window was across the bed, but it was boarded shut from the outside. So she was in a house, she surmised, but the house could be anywhere, in any city of any state.

Before she could try to hold on to the fading connection and tell Finn what she saw, the sound of a door opening broke her concentration. Snow looked to her right to see a man entering the room. The nausea returned at the sight of him as she remembered watching him approach her last night … was it last night? Snow realized with dread she had no idea how long she'd been unconscious.

The man stared at her from the doorway for a moment, his dark and eerily round eyes narrowed as they roved over her. He was thin but tall, deceptively strong, with slicked-back brown hair that touched his ears in greasy strands, sallow skin, and stained clothes. But she barely noticed that. All Snow could see was the memory of her abduction—the man who attacked her on campus, taking perverse pleasure in beating her, whispering in her ear during a bumpy car ride all the things he wanted to do to her. It was not a voice belonging to a man who knew mercy.

"Good," he spoke after taking a step forward and closing the door behind him. "You're already awake and waiting for me. It's not nearly as fun when you're asleep."

His response made her look down, and realize with dread and disgust she was wearing only a shirt and underwear. But she didn't feel pain there, like she thought she would if he … *No*, she tried to convince herself, *he's just trying to scare me.*

Snow tried to shrink back against the headboard as the man approached. If he noticed, his expression didn't change from that same glower of hardened calculation. He didn't stop until he was in front of her, arms crossed, mouth turning up into a cold smile.

"Who … who are you?" she managed to ask. Her voiced sounded breathy and terrified even though she'd tried hard to appear brave.

"Me? You can call me 'ole DU."

Just the name sent shivers through her. "Why are you doing this?"

His head tipped to the side as he considered her words. "Why?" he repeated with that creepy and predatory grin. "Because your daddy is a bad man, and since he didn't give me what I wanted," the man leaned down, eye level with Snow, "I'm going to take it from you."

Another whimper escaped before she could stop it.

"What do you mean? My father—"

"Thinks he can do what he does without suffering the consequences," her abductor finished.

Snow stared at him, frantically trying to figure out what he meant. Her father was a good man. He put the bad people away. Sure, there were times when he had to get information from some of those bad guys in order to put others in jail, but he had always assured her it was perfectly safe. That not talking to strangers was just a precaution.

Had he been lying to her all these years?

"What ... whatever he's done," Snow stammered, her mind racing with possibilities, "I'm sure he will do whatever you want to get me back."

DU reached out to trace a finger down her cheek, making a strange sound when she shuddered. "Maybe I don't want to give you back, my sweet little thing. Maybe I want to show him how very unhappy he's made me. But you..." His hand moved to the back of her neck and fisted in her hair. "You are going to make me very happy."

She tried to call to Finn, to tell him what this strange man said in hopes he could figure out what he meant, what her father had to do with why she was trapped in a cold room with an even colder kidnapper, but a fist connected with her cheekbone. Her thoughts were scattered, and, soon, faded into a black curtain that blocked the beating her body was forced to endure.

They booked a cheap motel for the night somewhere in Pennsylvania, Finn unable to drive any farther without his head dropping in exhaustion and Joe refusing to take the lead without a night's sleep. The motel was tucked away a few miles from the highway, next to a fast food joint where they got their dinner, choosing to eat in the privacy of their room.

"So," Joe began while unwrapping his burger, "wanna tell me more about this grand quest of yours?"

"Not 'til you tell me the real reason why Charlie sent you along. We both know I don't need a babysitter. I only said it mainly to throw him off."

Joe eyed the younger man while taking a bite, chewing slowly. "You think Charlie don't see right through that? He knew you're gonna get yourself killed by yourself and would have sent me along even without your little suggestion. I know it too."

"You don't even know what I'm doing."

"Don't need to know what you're doing to know you ain't got the smarts to pull it off solo."

The reply irritated Finn, though he tried not to show it. He had to keep Joe thinking he was welcome. The last thing he needed was the lackey running back to Charlie and saying something that would have his ass dragged back home. Finn chose not to reply and dug into his food.

But Charlie's number two wasn't so intent on letting the issue go. "You gonna make me ask again?"

Shooting a glare across the table, Finn chewed slowly, deliberately, giving himself time to think. In the rush to get ready earlier he hadn't actually thought through the lie he would tell Joe. It was a miracle he hadn't asked during the ride south already.

"If you make me—"

"I got a girl I've been after who finally agreed to give it up," Finn cut in, lifting a shoulder to appear nonchalant.

"She moved a couple years back for school but we kept in touch. What can I say, my charm works across state borders."

Joe scoffed and shook his head. "You telling me you're driving all the way Georgia for some ass?"

"Is it really that hard to believe? If you're good, maybe I'll even let you have a taste when I'm done with her." It sickened him to even suggest such a thing.

Leaning back, Joe pointed a fry at Finn. "First off, we both know I'd take the first taste. Ain't no way I'm gettin' some punk's sloppy seconds. Second, I ain't buyin' it. Everyone knows you're stuck on that cute little black-haired number always sneakin' in back to see you. What's her name, Leo's kid. So let's try again. You bullshit me again, I got Charlie on speed dial."

Busted, deciding against attempting another lie to a man who was trained to get information out of people, Finn relented and pulled out his phone, clicking through a few Google searches until he finally landed on a Georgia news page. And there, front and center on his screen, was a picture of Snow. This one was different than the image he saw before, a typical school picture. The image now was a candid shot. She was looking just above the camera and smiling wide, perhaps laughing at something the person on the other side said. Her golden hair framed her face in a halo, the sun lighting up her porcelain skin.

Local College Student Abducted from Campus, read the headline.

The search continues for two men involved in the disappearance of a young woman, continued the first line of the article.

It was public now, which meant not only did Finn

have more information to go on, but he also had Snow's real name. If he was a smarter man, he could have done a simple computer search to find out everything about her. If he was a more trusting man, he could have gone to an expert and asked for a favor. But he wasn't a smarter or trusting man. All he had was the drive and willingness to slice open whoever hurt her. That, and the knowledge that prying too deep would likely alert the abductors that someone was after them, which would put Snow in even more danger.

No, he had to go in slow and under the radar, as difficult as that was.

"This is why we're going to Atlanta." Finn slid the phone across the small table to Joe. "That's her, my friend I said needed help. She was kidnapped two days ago walking home from campus. Police don't know anything yet, but I'm going to find her, and I'm going to get her home."

Joe stared down at the phone, moving the screen up and down with one finger, forehead furrowed. "How you gonna find some chick when no one knows nothin' and there ain't no clues in the news?"

"I ... have my ways." When Joe lifted a brow, Finn merely shrugged. "You and Charlie aren't the only ones with resources." He took his phone back and stood to throw his trash away. "I'm going to bed."

They both knew it was to avoid further questioning, but luckily Joe didn't protest. After a few minutes both were in their respective beds—Joe insisted they book a single room with double beds, which Finn knew was another way to keep an eye on him. Despite his exhaustion and his body's desire to give in to the surprisingly comfortable bed and pillow molding to him, Finn found his mind racing.

He was worried. Though he felt Snow in the back of his mind, it was a weak manifestation, like a memory he couldn't quite remember. And, worse, he couldn't hear her. Part of him feared he'd imagined her calling his name, that maybe he'd brought on the nausea himself out of panic and his whispered name a mere wish for her safety. But just as soon as he wondered it, he convinced himself it had to be Snow. Her aura was familiar, distraught as it was.

I know you're with me, Snow-Glow. Hold on for me, okay?

Sleep tugged at his eyes, dropping them closed as he continued his tormented thoughts. Where was Snow? What was she doing—what was being done to her? Was she okay? Would she be able to talk to him again, give him clues as to her whereabouts?

Tomorrow morning he would scour the news for more information, search for some piece of information, no matter how big or small, he could use along the way to Georgia. He could only hope that, wherever she was, Snow could hold on just a little bit longer.

CHAPTER 15

H E SAID TO hold on. He sent her his strength, his
courage. But it wasn't enough.

Snow laid on her side on the bumpy mattress,
arms and legs listless, eyes staring vacantly at the wall.
The thin beam of light around the boarded-up window told
her it was daytime. When was the last time she slept?
She'd watched the light change as it played across the wall
for hours. If she tried hard enough, she could focus on the
shadows as they moved and block out what was happening
around her, to her, and pretend she didn't exist at all.

But, try as she might, Snow couldn't make the
sounds, smells, sights of this horrible room disappear.
They enveloped and suffocated her. They made her weak.
She'd always thought herself to be so smart, yet she
couldn't think of a way out. So strong, yet they had taken
her will, the fight for her soul, within days. Shame flooded
her veins.

A princess would never feel ashamed. Even as the thought crossed her mind, Snow followed it with another. *Stupid, stupid girl. Grow up already.*

Once, in another life, dreams of being a princess weren't so foolish. Far-fetched, perhaps, but innocent, every little girl's fantasy to one day grow up and live in a castle with a man who loved her so much he would slay dragons to save her. Snow could remember playing with Amelia, who would sometimes indulge her with a few hours of dressing up dolls, though her disdain for girly things always showed through.

It helped to think about such childhood things, focusing on memory rather than present, so Snow chose a specific day—her eleventh birthday. Amelia thought she was too old for a princess party, and maybe she was, but for a little girl who grew up with nothing, one day where she was royalty was the most perfect day of them all.

"No princess is complete without her tiara," her mother had said the morning of her party, placing a silver plastic tiara atop a young Snow's head. Brimming with excitement, Snow had raced to the mirror above her dresser, admiring her crown from every angle. There were green and pink stones all along the sides, with one big, clear, oval-shaped gem in the center. It sparkled in the light, making her look and feel like a true fancy lady.

"I'm a real princess now," she had proclaimed as she stood straight and tall like royalty would do. She lifted a hand in a regal wave. *"A princess who talks to animals and sings songs that make everyone happy."*

"So lame." From the doorway, Amelia had scoffed, tossing back her long hair dismissively. *"Princesses are so girly."*

Snow remembered sticking her tongue out and adjusting her tiara. *"You're just jealous that I'm the prettiest of them all and will live happily ever after with my prince."*

There was no such thing as happily ever after. There were no princes and princesses, only plastic tiaras to make little girls think they were more important than they really were in the world. Doubt and hate shattered her cheerful memory, lifting Snow back into the now. *Princesses are for babies. Happily ever after is for morons.*

Don't say that, Snow-Glow.

No. She couldn't let Finn be here, not now, not in this moment. Snow squeezed her eyes shut, blanking her mind, her emotions, her thoughts. Deep in her mind she could feel him searching for the truth of her present, for clues, but the truth was too awful a burden to bear.

Stop it, Snow. Stop pushing me away. Let me help you.

She wanted him to go away. If he knew what was happening, it would be too embarrassing to bear.

Snow, talk to me. Tell me where you are.

She didn't know where she was. She didn't know anything except her father was somehow involved and a man named DU took pleasure in making her scream. What good was it to take comfort in Finn coming for her, if no one knew where she was, including her?

Answer me, Snow. I'm right here. Talk to me.

He wasn't right here. She was alone in the cold room with nothing but the light and shadows on the wall to accompany her.

She couldn't stop the unrelenting abuse or the stifling loneliness, but she could, just this once, stop Finn from feeling it. *I'm sorry, Finn-Monster. I can't let you suffer too.*

She'd shut him out. From her thoughts, from what she was feeling, from everything.

The worst part was, he understood why. He knew what it was like to have secrets and need to keep them. But this secret was too big and he needed to be part of it, which was why he had locked himself in the single-stall gas station bathroom hours after getting back on the road, sitting on the sticky floor with his back to the wall and headphones in his ears to block out the rest of the world.

"Talk to me, Snow," he said to himself as he leaned his head back and closed his eyes, concentrating on the static in his head. Never before did he have to work so hard to find her. It had always been so easy in the past, a simple flicking of a switch to connect with Snow and have a conversation. Other times he didn't have to do anything at all. Her voice just appeared in his head.

"Come on, Snow."

Sounds of the gas station disappeared—the hum of the beer cooler on the other side of the wall, the dulled voices in conversation, the steady drip of a leaky sink. *Where are you, Snow? Talk to me*, he said on repeat in his head, waiting for a response each time and getting nothing. She wasn't talking.

"Fine," he muttered, now almost angry with her refusal to let him in. His eyes opened and searched the bathroom as he considered other ways to connect, not really seeing anything until they landed on a piece of metal by the trash can. Retrieving it, Finn stared down at the scrap metal, a cold slab of steel with thin, jagged edges. It might have once been part of a pipe, or maybe some kind of frame. Whatever it once was, its future was destined for something else. Already Finn could envision its potential.

"Focus, dumbass." His fingers closed around the metal, offering a small slice of comfort as he again turned his thoughts to Snow. "All right. You don't wanna talk, then I'm gonna feel." Changing tracks, he stopped listening for her voice and instead tried to center himself so he could hone in on her emotions.

His fingers worked over the steel as he concentrated, taking long breaths with slow exhales, imagining his soul lifting from his body. It took a few minutes, but he felt it— a prickling of his skin as it felt unfamiliar surroundings. The hard concrete against his back softened into a lumpy mattress. His feet chilled as though his boots never covered them. The smell of smoke and blood filled his nostrils, as the taste of bile hit his tongue. And parts of his body hurt that should never ache. Bones felt broken, his back burned, every part of his face swollen.

What had they done to her?

Finn didn't let himself rage. He kept his own emotions in check, finding it easier to do the more he kept his concentration. He could feel Snow's sorrow and her desire to give up. But there was something else too, a determination and will to live she hadn't discovered yet.

You're strong, Snow. You just have to feel it.

He owes a debt he can't pay.

The man's voice nearly startled Finn out of his focus. It was so clear, it seemed the other person was sitting right next to him. He wondered if Snow had fallen asleep, her barriers down and allowing him open access. Whatever it was, he took advantage of his ability to eavesdrop.

He's in over his head, the man was saying, likely to another of Snow's abductors. *He knows we have her and what we will do.*

Silence—another person speaking, he wondered—before, *He was given a choice. Pay his debt, or give us the girl and all would be forgiven.*

Who cares how long she lasts? As long as I get what I want, it doesn't matter what happens. Don't worry. You'll get your chance with her and her sister.

Sister. The word resounded in Finn's head. These men weren't going to stop with Snow. They would go after her sister as well, and their father was doing nothing to stop it. And why? Because he owed a debt? But what kind?

Banging on the door ripped Finn from Snow's world. His heart began to race at the intrusion and he realized he was shivering despite the heat in the bathroom.

"What the fuck are you doing!" Joe called from the other side. "I've been waitin' out there for twenty minutes! Get the fuck out!"

Grumbling to himself, Finn stood and took a moment to compose himself. All the things Snow felt were gone, replaced by his own environment, but he still felt off. Overwhelmed and tired, but also at a loss. He learned nothing new. Not where Snow was, not who took her. Just that her abductors had no intention of letting her go.

"I'm coming!" he yelled back when Joe pounded on the door again. Shoving the piece of steel in his pocket, Finn wrenched the door open and shoved past the man, stomping out to the car and getting in the passenger side. "You're driving."

"Oh, I'm drivin'," Joe replied, sarcasm thick. But he got in the driver's seat and started the ignition, then turned to Finn. "What the fuck happened in there? You got some kind of stomach shit or you in there plottin' against me?"

Exasperated, Finn shook his head and raked a hand through messy, unwashed hair. "Why are you always thinking I'm plotting against you?"

"'Cause I know you. Always wantin' more jobs. *My* jobs. Thinking your connection with Charlie will get you special treatment."

Finn laughed at that. "Special treatment? I still get the shit jobs, Joe. Don't act like you're on the way out."

"Damn right I'm not." Joe nodded and shoved the car into drive. "I'm takin' over when the old man retires. You keep that in mind."

"Whatever you say."

With a roll of his eyes, Finn opened a bag of chips and shoved a few in his mouth. He stared out the window at the passing trees as they got back on the highway. They'd be stopping soon to sleep, both of them exhausted, Finn needing to recharge if he was going to be anywhere close to useful when he finally found Snow. He thought about the connection made earlier, going over and over each feeling, each word, trying to glean something new.

"What's with you and those stupid things, anyway?"

Once again pulled from his thoughts, Finn glanced over at Joe, who motioned with his head. Finn looked down at his lap. He'd torn the chip bag into strips and was wrapping them around an old pen one by one. With the silver trunk and green pieces arching off the plastic, the piece vaguely resembled a tree.

"Don't know," he answered Joe. "Just like making them."

"What for? What's the point?"

Finn shrugged. "Keeps my hands busy, I guess." Embarrassed by the scrutiny, he tossed the pen-tree to the floorboard. "Find us a cheap motel. We'll stop for the night and get an early start, get in Georgia by morning."

The car was silent, Joe stealing glances over at his passenger every now and then. "You're a weird kid," he finally said. "Makin' all those doll things, hangin' out in gas station bathrooms."

"So?"

"So, just know that I'm watchin' you. If this trip is anythin' other than to find some chick, I'll put a bullet in you myself."

You can try, Finn thought wryly. But to Joe he said, "Good thing it's all for some chick then, huh?" then settled back, tuning the other man out the rest of the drive.

CHAPTER 16

B LOOD DRIPPED FROM her nose, matching the water steadily seeping from the ceiling. On the floor, Snow drew her legs up to her chest and rested her head upon them, her body starting to rock. She hurt so badly, in every part of her right down to her toes.

"What did I do?" she whispered, needing to hear a voice in the silence of this terrifying house, needing the comfort of something familiar even if she couldn't answer all the questions swimming in her mind. "Why is this happening?"

Tears leaked from the corners of her closed eyes as her mind forced her to remember all the horrible things it had experienced. The man, who'd identified himself only as DU, had taken from her every scream, every plea, she had left. Never before had she known she could be in so much pain, that her body could take so much and still allow her heart to beat.

Through every punch, every open-handed slap, every foot to her ribs, every ... force she wasn't strong enough to verbalize, she continued to curse her family, her father. Snow knew her father came across bad people in his line of work. In fact, his work was the reason why she feared strangers for so long, always being warned not to trust anyone she didn't know personally, because there were always bad people who might want to take revenge on her family. But never did she imagine those bad people actually would come after her, all to get back at her father.

"Please make it stop, Daddy," she said into her knees, hoping, praying, that if DU really did want revenge, then he'd at least put up a ransom so the police would know who had her, and how to save her. But what if he didn't? What if her father really was involved with bad people like DU suggested, and *couldn't* go to the police? She couldn't fathom the possibility.

Her rocking was interrupted by the door opening. Snow refused to look, instead choosing to pretend if she ignored DU, he wouldn't see her tucked between the wall and bed, trying hard to be invisible. When a large, strong hand wrapped around her wrist, she knew her pretending had been in vain.

Snow whimpered when she was yanked to her feet. Each movement set her ribcage on fire and reminded her where every single bruise colored her pale skin. But she didn't protest. That just made it worse.

"Miss me?" DU asked with a grin, lips parting to reveal two rows of yellow teeth. He tossed her on the bed.

"Please don't," Snow begged timidly, not sure what she was asking him not to do but knowing it would be awful.

DU barely looked at her. He busied himself with a bag she hadn't realized he brought in, setting a few items down on the table next to the bed. With no small amount of horror she watched him take a syringe out, followed by items she couldn't identify. He was going to kill her, she realized. After everything he'd done, all that talk about her father, he wouldn't let her live. Whatever that substance was, it would mean her death if it got inside her.

What would Finn do? Snow searched deep inside herself for the connection to her male counterpart, needing his courage, something she had lacked her entire life.

Finn would be brave. He would fight, fight to the death if need be, but he wouldn't let these thugs take him down easily. He would be smart and fearless and not wait on anyone to be his hero.

He would survive.

But how? A quick survey of the room had a plan formulating—DU on the other side of the bed prepping his syringe while muttering profane things to her beneath his breath, the boarded-up window offering no escape, the unguarded bedroom door beckoning to her.

Gathering every bit of adrenaline she had and ignoring the jabs of pain throughout her body, Snow launched herself off the bed, bare feet landing surprisingly solidly on the floor. *Run.*

She didn't let herself think about the consequences, only run, run as fast as she possibly could. The door was thrown open to the sound of DU's furious shout at her back. But still she ran, pushing off the opposite wall and tearing down the narrow hallway, eyes frantically searching for a way out.

A kitchen with dishes piled high. A bathroom that

hadn't been cleaned in possibly forever. Messy living room with clutter her weak legs easily jumped over. There—a door that could only lead outside, and a window next to it, curtain partially open to reveal a quiet street with woods lining the other side.

Her hand had just grabbed the doorknob when an arm wrapped around her waist and dragged her backward. Tightening her grip, Snow refused to break away from her escape, yanking as hard as she could only to be pulled away with one rough jerk. When the last finger slipped off the cool metal, Snow began to scream as loud as she could to anyone who might be listening.

"Shut the fuck up!" DU slapped a hand across her mouth, momentarily stunning her, and hauled Snow away, back to the room where she was being kept prisoner. Snow continued to thrash, refusing to go quietly. She didn't know where her sudden courage came from but she used it as best she could, only feeling it fade when DU threw her on the bed.

"Stay the fuck there!" he shouted, his fist connecting with her jaw when she made to run again. "So this is how you want to play."

Head still spinning from the hit, she watched in horror as he ripped off his belt, and tried to squirm out of his grasp when he took hold of her wrist, but he was too strong and soon her entire arm and wrist were strapped to the headboard. Already she was looking for a way to re-move the belt and he knew it, and wasted no time wrench-ing her other arm behind her back and securing it with a zip tie.

"You want to make this worse?" he asked, his face so close she could feel his breath as he spoke. He stayed there until she shook her head. "Didn't think so." Moving back to his bag of supplies, DU took his time, drawing out her torture and leaving her to wonder what he as planning.

She didn't have to wonder long. Though Snow considered herself fairly sheltered, she had watched enough movies to know he was preparing a drug. And because he clearly intended to inject it, she could only guess it was heroin. "Please don't," she whispered, hating that her voice broke and she was once again back to the scared little girl with no courage. "If you just tell my dad what you want, I know he'll—"

"He'll what?" DU turned, a knowing grin crossing his thin face. "Give me money? Meet my demands?"

"Well … yes," Snow replied, confused as to his expression.

DU picked up the syringe, filling it with his concoction. "I have made my demands quite clear."

"You've talked to my dad?"

"In a manner of speaking."

The hope that had been building in her chest died at his response. Snow could only watch as DU rounded the bed, easily avoiding her legs as she kicked out, and wrapped rubber tubing around her upper arm. "No," she protested when the needle approached her skin, grimacing when it pierced through. It didn't take long to feel its effects, and even as the narcotic threatened to embrace her in its grasp, she had to ask, "Why?"

DU pulled the needle out and pointed at her with it. "Because it's fun, buttercup." He laughed as her head lolled to the side. "Because until I get what I want, I'm gonna make sure your daddy knows what happens when he fucks with the wrong people."

His hand reached up, fingers grasping her chin and lifting her head so she was forced to look at him. Her vision blurred, but his words were crystal clear as they echoed around her skull. "And look how much fun it is, to taint his perfect little girl."

She didn't know when he left, or if he even did. Snow was trapped in the grip of this strange euphoric high unlike anything she'd ever experienced before. It terrified her how much she enjoyed it. It made the pain go away, made her panic fade. Nothing else existed except for this feeling.

No. She struggled to maintain her senses, not entirely sure if she was actually moving her head or just imagining it. The battle exhausted her, a physical and mental pain.

Ride it, Snow.

Finn's voice crept into her presence. At first she didn't understand his command, until she felt her control slip and more euphoria flooded through her. Yes, ride it, indeed.

Let it take away your pain.

It took away everything. The pain, the fear, the desire to escape. She didn't need anything except the ride.

When you come back, I'll be there for you.

Finn was on his way. She didn't need to worry. Her protector would soon come and take her away, to the place where she could be happy again.

Closing her eyes, Snow let herself ride away the night.

———

Their day started early the next morning, getting back on the road by eight. Finn was determined to get to Atlanta by noon and start his search while there was still daylight. His plan was to spend the entire drive trying to connect with Snow, so he'd at least have a place to begin.

The road tunneled before him, a steady passing of trees and cars. Finn let it all pass by in a blur. His mind focused on his connection with Snow, weak as it was, trying to not only hear her but sense her locations as he'd been able to do yesterday morning.

Come on, Snow, he called out to her. His hands tightened on the steering wheel when he didn't get a response. Next to him, Joe rummaged around in his bag before pulling out a magazine about guns and ammo. *Snow!*

Fucking answer me!

The silent shout did nothing but anger and scare him. She'd always answered in the past, especially when he cussed. She'd made it her mission to "clean his mouth up," as she liked to tell him. The quiet in his head was confusing—he knew she was alive, he could feel her, but why wouldn't she answer?

Because she couldn't, he told himself, thinking back to what he'd felt the day before. Sick, aching, frightened. He knew that feeling. She'd been beaten, badly. And worse ... Things he couldn't think of right now, things she'd spared him from by blocking him out. The only way she could, would, answer him was through her senses.

Let me feel you, Snow, he tried again, inhaling deeply, blinking a few times, calming his nerves all in hopes of tuning in to his abducted friend.

Nothing. A gaping void of black air consumed him. Finn let out a heavy breath as the complete sense of *nothing* threatened to tear him apart. He couldn't live like this, with such despair and loneliness inside him. The weakness infuriated him. He was supposed to be tough, a rogue bad-ass able to take care of himself. So why was he so fucking dependent on some girl being with him?

Because she wasn't just some girl, he answered his own question. It was Snow, his other half. His better half. He wasn't a whole person without her, never had been. And right now, the only way he could help his better half was by giving her the courage to help herself.

In the past they transferred their energy and emotions by accident. It had to be deliberate, a fast and intentional gift of bravery. He focused on the feel of her, picturing his courage leaving him in a visible thread and entering her, fueling her.

And then, a flicker of something in his chest. Finn shifted in his seat, honing in on the sensation, one hand rubbing at the spot. It built, an explosion of panic laced with determination as his heart began to race. His breath shortened, arms and legs twitching with the need to run.

Run.

Snow was running, and he could feel it, a whole-body takeover as her block against him lowered and their senses united. Bare feet on carpet, hands touching the cold metal of a doorknob—a flash of woods and an empty street just beyond a splintered window frame and filmy glass. A trailer replaced the car, woods overshadowing other vehicles on the road. The entire world shifted as his mind let itself be transported. But just as soon as he saw life through Snow's eyes the vision disappeared, replaced by the highway.

"You're thinking awfully hard," Joe commented from the passenger seat.

His concentration broken by the sudden voice, Finn

felt Snow's presence slip away. He resented being brought out of the moment and it took him a minute to clear his thoughts and slow his racing heart before he was able to reply. "Just … preparing myself."

"For what, exactly?" Joe waited, but Finn didn't offer further explanation. "Saving the damsel in distress even though you ain't got a clue where to find her?" When Finn didn't answer, he continued, "You ever think that maybe I could be of assistance here? Course, you'd have to tell me the truth about this little charade of yours."

He didn't want to tell Joe the truth. It felt too personal to give up his secret, a betrayal of sorts. But he could give some version of the truth, as Joe did know his way around the streets. "Fine," Finn relented, sucking in a deep breath, knowing he was delaying as he tried to think of a way to word the past thirteen years of his life.

"I've been friends with this girl since I was a kid. She's not a girlfriend, just a friend. I don't talk about her because she's different than us. She's good, innocent, sheltered. She wanted to be a doctor."

"How the hell you end up with a friend like that?"

"It just happened." Finn shrugged, keeping his eyes on the road so he wouldn't have to look at his passenger. All the while he tried to reconnect with Snow. "Some bad shit happened, and now it's my job to protect her and make it right."

Joe frowned, fingers tapping on his thigh as he listened. "And she lives all the way down in Georgia? How do you know she was kidnapped? Were you on the phone with her when it happened?"

"No."

"Then how do you know? 'Cause you saw somethin'

about it on your phone?" When Finn didn't answer, Joe looked over, eyes narrowed. "Do you know where or why they took her?"

"No."

"Do you know who took her?"

"No. All I know is it's a guy with tattoos on his arms and another skinny guy with dark hair."

Joe was quiet a beat before asking, "You see that on the news?"

"No. I just know it."

Each answer earned another dubious leer. "So you just know all this stuff no one else knows. Except where she is. Then how the hell you gonna find her?"

"I have my ways."

"Right." Joe snorted and shook his head. "Your *ways*. You always were a punk. Who is this chick really, kid? This just some girl you saw on the news and you decided to be the big hero, prove yourself to Charlie? You tryin' to take my place?"

Finn rolled his eyes, but Joe wasn't finished. "I'll ask you one more time. Who exactly is this girl?"

"I already told you." There was an edge to his voice now, one that matched Joe's. "She's my friend, more family than anyone else back home. It's my job to protect her, so that's what I'm gonna do. If you think I'm just gonna forget about her, pretend nothing happened, then you really are a fucking idiot." His icy eyes turned to Joe, who was staring at him with no small amount of suspicion. "I'm gonna find the fucker who did this to her, and I'm going to kill him."

He considered Joe's silence a victory. Finn turned back to the road, wanting nothing more than to continue his tirade, but his determination faded. Instead, warmth spread through him. A sensation he'd only felt a few times before, but one he would always recognize as the slow burn of an impending high. It consumed him, clouded his mind, turned his limbs into liquid, excited him as much as it did terrify. Finn vaguely heard Joe shouting at him as the car began to swerve, but it was too late. He was lost in the high.

This was different, though. He wasn't just lost in the feeling, in the euphoria of floating for as long as he could. There was fear, too, and pain, a physical battle of will. His subconscious didn't want to enjoy it and was fighting the warmth, terrified of losing control, even as fire-hot pokers jabbed at his stomach and head.

Ride it, Snow, he managed to think, feeling his thoughts scatter in a thousand different directions. It was the only thing he could think against the rush. *Let it take away your pain. When you come back, I'll be there for you.*

CHAPTER 17

H E WAS LOST in oblivion. Surrounded by blurs of color, bound to an empty existence where thought and focus and worry were but distant memories floating away on a warm breeze, Finn was free. There was nowhere he had to be, no pain of another's to feel, just … calm, peaceful freedom.

He floated for hours, days, months—time no longer mattered. There was no need to rush here. Finn had forgotten how much he loved the drop into nothing. It had been a rare thing for him to indulge in the high, not wanting to end up like his mother, but now he wondered why he'd ever turned a cold shoulder.

This was the escape he craved, from his past, his present, and certainly the bloody future awaiting him. It gave him total awareness of his soul, of the soft cotton against his chest, the cool piece of steel in his pocket, the oils starting to coat unwashed hair, even the sound of traffic and chirping birds as they echoed in his ears.

Pressure against his chest made him stir, trying to pull him out of unconsciousness. He couldn't break through the surface of his daze. He didn't *want* to break through. A roaring in his ears had him turning his head side to side, trying to determine the source of the noise, force it to be quiet and let him enjoy his peaceful ride into the void. Still, fragments of conversation trickled in, angrily spoken demands he didn't understand.

I expect ... You owe me ... I will kill ... You knew what would happen if you ...Not such a good girl any-more...

A man's voice, muffled as though being heard through a wall. A man's voice talking about Snow.

Snow. It came back to Finn then—his purpose, his destiny, his reason for leaving home. He was supposed to save her, not become the person he hated most in the world.

Debts have to be paid. The man was speaking again. But who was he talking to?

Iron Creek ... Estates.

A different interruption into his drug-fueled haze. A young woman's voice, whispering to him slowly. Snow's voice, interrupted by breathy gasps.

Even in his state of twilight, Finn zeroed in on Snow. Yes, he could feel her now. Groggy. Exhausted and weak. Struggling to reach out to him as they both slowly awoke from their stupor. *Iron Creek Estates?* he repeated, trying to understand. *Is that where you are?*

He's ... talking to someone ... wants payment ... one way or another ... to meet him at ... Estates.

Are you there now? In the house I saw? Did you try to

escape?

...House? Her response was unsure, and so quiet he could barely hear her. *Finn? I'm so tired.*

Stay with me, Snow. Snow? he called to her when she didn't answer, and again, his voice growing louder as hers lowered. Finally, after long and painful moments wondering where she went, he heard her once more.

Please help me, Finn.

———

The plea jolted Finn awake. He leapt to his feet in one fluid motion, head swiveling to either side when he didn't recognize his surroundings. Some kind of room—bed in the corner, bathroom along the same wall, scratched-up dresser with his leather jacket tossed on top, TV playing an old sitcom rerun.

Finally his gaze landed on Joe sitting in an ugly orange chair, watching TV. "Where are we?"

"Crossed the border a few hours ago," he answered plainly, eyes never leaving the television. "I was tired of drivin' your ass around, figured I'd get a room and let you sleep off whatever the fuck you took."

"Took?" Finn ran a hand through his hair, thinking back to the last thing he remembered. Talking to Snow, feeling what she felt as she ran—trying to escape, he could only assume—then ... warmth. It all happened so quickly. He didn't take anything. Not that he could remember, anyway.

"What happened?"

"You tell me, kid." Joe took a drink from a bottle on the floor next to him, then used it to gesture at Finn. "You

passed out, about took us out on the middle of the highway, not to mention the other cars. Tossed your ass in the
backseat once I got us off the road, then took over. So,
here we wait."

Perplexed, Finn sat on the edge of the bed, half
tempted to grab the bottle and down it in three long swallows. He resisted only because he refused to be like his
mother and solve all of life's problems with a drink.

"I didn't take anything," he managed to say around
his bewilderment. "I ... Maybe I'm getting sick."

"You were mumbling something in your sleep. Iron
Creek Estates." Joe waited a beat, then added, "Something
you want to tell me?"

Instead of answering, Finn pulled out his phone. "Iron
Creek Estates," he repeated to himself beneath his breath.
The few words Snow was able to utter spoke volumes.
While he didn't know who all was involved or what house
she was in, it didn't matter, because he knew where she
was.

Typing in the neighborhood name, Finn frantically
searched for the setting, checking all of Georgia, foot tapping impatiently. When the map finally zeroed in on the
location, he frowned. "I don't understand."

"Well that makes two of us."

Finn shot an irritated glance over at Joe before returning his attention to his phone, convinced he was doing
something wrong. But, no, every search engine he checked
told him there was no Iron Creek Estates in Georgia.

He knew he'd heard her correctly. Snow's voice was
distinctive, always clear and present in his mind. And,
thanks to his strengthening connection with her, he also
knew her abductor, whoever he was, had some kind of is-

sue with her father. Probably money, he figured, but another quick online search would hopefully reveal more about her family, and maybe what they had to do with the location where Snow was being held. Surely by this point the cops—and therefore the news stations—knew something, if Snow's father had been brought into negotiations.

"You've got to be kidding me." Jumping to his feet, Finn scanned an article, then another, scrolling through black words on a white screen until they all blurred together.

Nothing. There was nothing on a ransom, on any demands being made to Snow's family. Only an update on her kidnapping informing the public the search was still on, a call for help in finding the men responsible, and a picture to remind anyone watching who to look for.

"That mother fucker didn't tell the cops."

"Who didn't tell the cops what?" At Joe's wary question, Finn spun around and all but launched the phone at him. Joe caught the phone and spent a minute scrolling. "What is this? There's nothin' there."

"Exactly." Feeling vindicated, Finn began to pace. "There's nothing there about Snow's parents, which means whoever this asshole is who took her, he's talking to them on the side and cops haven't been brought in. And all this time she thought her family was good."

"Snow?" Joe repeated after a moment's hesitation. "Your girl's name is Snow?"

Finn paused mid-step, only now realizing her name had slipped out. Too late to take it back, he figured, and pushed on. "It's a nickname because she likes princesses. And that's not the point. The point is that her father clearly is trying to handle this on his own. Maybe it's a deal gone bad or he pissed off the wrong person, I don't know. I don't know what he does that would have him involved with these people. But I do know that if I don't get to her soon, this guy might take it a step further. I have to get to her, now."

Joe watched as the younger man grabbed a pen and pad of paper on the nightstand next to the bed and started drawing a rough sketch of what looked like the inside of a house. Finn was so wrapped up in his drawing he didn't notice Joe pull out his cell phone, subtly press a button, then another, keeping his arm down at his side as he said, "So, you have to get to her ... at Iron Creek Estates."

"Right."

"Because even though the cops and the news have no idea where she is, you do."

Finn looked up from his drawing, hearing the suspicion in Joe's voice. "Right," he said again, slowly this time.

"How do you *know* she's there? How do you know this guy wants something from her father? You didn't know anything yesterday, and all of a sudden you now have an exact location. You ain't left my side since we left and you been out cold for hours. But now you know where this girl is."

Joe stood and crossed his arms. "I don't buy it. There's somethin' you're not telling me. Especially since you said she was in Atlanta, and now you're sayin' she's in Iron Creek Estates. There ain't a neighborhood like that anywhere in near Atlanta. I checked. You're up to somethin'."

"Atlanta was before I knew exactly where she was," Finn shot back, seeing the debate quickly sliding from his control. "I needed a place to start. Plan's changed."

"Oh, no," Joe drawled, fingers tapping against his biceps, "I think this was your plan all along. Just took me a little long to catch on is all."

They engaged in a standoff, one knowing there was more to the truth than being told, the other refusing to reveal anything further. Finn's mind raced with ways to overtake the older, stronger, much more brutal man, each idea coming up short.

He couldn't tell Joe how he knew where Snow was, just as he couldn't quite figure out what "plan" Joe thought he had secretly cooked up. There was just one purpose to this trip—avenge Snow. And if he wanted to do just that, he'd have to ditch Charlie's chosen henchman.

The only problem was, Joe was standing between him and the door. There was no way out of this room.

But he refused to show fear or any sort of trepidation. Straightening his shoulders, Finn took a step forward and kept his glare even. "Get out of my way, Joe."

"Not until you tell me what exactly your game is here." Joe's stance shifted threateningly—feet braced, shoulders set, chin held high. "All that mutterin' in your sleep, sayin' things you shouldn't be sayin' if you wanted to keep things secret. You blew it at Iron Creek Estates. You and me both know that only means one thing. You better start talking right fucking now."

"And if I don't?" Finn crossed his arms as well, then lifted a brow when there was a sharp knock at the door. "Saved by the bell," he said sarcastically, but Joe didn't seem fazed.

"You sure about that, kid?"

Finn watched Joe walk backward to the door, keeping

a wary eye on him as he let their guest in. As soon as he saw who was on the other side of the door, Finn's heart thumped painfully in his chest, his stomach clutching and bile burning in his throat. He didn't, couldn't, speak as the man entered, his lanky frame filling the doorway, a black shadow against the brilliant afternoon sun.

The visitor stepped inside, letting the light reveal the sharp angles of his thin face, the dark hue of greasy, slicked-back brown hair, the jaunt of bony shoulders padded by an oversized beige windbreaker. Through round glasses peered predatory eyes, zeroing in on the young man next to the bed who instantly remembered his name.

But Finn wouldn't let his expression, his stance, show how much his body was trembling on the inside.

"You remember 'ole DU, don't ya, kid?"

Childhood memories flooded through Finn, too many years remembering what had been done to him, what others had let happen. His breath caught in his chest at the visions swimming behind his eyes. Yes, he remembered 'ole DU, the man who rarely went by his given name of Duane and preferred the nickname. Finn shuddered internally, knowing what those letters stood for.

Still, he made damn sure his voice was smooth when he replied, "Sure. One of Ma's dickhead meal tickets."

He'd expected his opponent to snap back, launch into a fight. That would have been welcome. Something he could easily handle. Finn wasn't prepared for the slow smirk that crossed DU's face, nor could he look away from those long, callused hands as they slid down to grip his belt buckle, fingers tapping on the jeans just below. A suggestion, a warning—a promise that threatened to suck the courage out of Finn even as he fought to maintain his façade.

How humiliating it was to know that after all these years, he was just the scared little boy trapped in his room, another one of his mother's dealers pissed off she didn't have the cash and taking payment however he saw fit.

Payment. It hit him then, something Snow had whispered to him before she faded away followed by her abductor's claim.

Debts have to be paid.

His eyes moved from DU's hands to Joe's knowing glower. "I didn't pass out," he whispered, trying to piece things together but only getting as far as that one fact. "You did something to me … How … Why?"

DU took a step forward, enough to close the door, as Joe replied, "You really do have balls of steel, kid. You had me going for a while there, actin' like you were playing hero to some long-lost friend. I knew somethin' was up, knew it for sure when you let it slip who your little suspects were."

Finn's brow furrowed as he tried to recall what was said. When Joe shifted, his eyes were drawn to the pictures inked on his arms. And then he remembered telling Joe who took Snow—a man with tattoos and another with dark, slicked-back hair.

"Where is she?" An animalistic rage drew Finn closer. "What the fuck is going on?"

Joe leveled a steely glare at him. "I should be askin' you that same question."

It quickly became obvious he would get no answers out of Joe, so Finn answered them on his own. "Looks like Charlie's reach goes farther than I thought it did. How many people are in debt to him? To you? Why did you bring her into this?"

Joe's eyes narrowed as he considered the question. He glanced over at DU, whose unwavering stare never left the boy in front of them, before replying on a shrug, "You said it yourself. Debts had to be paid."

Pure, unadulterated fury consumed Finn. He lunged at Joe, who blocked the attempt with the mere wave of his muscle arm, sending Finn tumbling into the chair. Spinning around, he readied to attack again. "Where is she!"

"Oh, boy, you already know the answer to that."

DU's voice slicked over Finn's flesh, a sticky coating of shame that weighed him down. He'd heard that voice too many times, tried hard to forget it after so many nights praying deep down the man would stay gone after skipping town more than a decade ago.

But he wasn't that little boy anymore, Finn told himself, He was twenty goddamn years old, with a reputation to match his place in Charlie's organization. Cops knew better than to fuck with him. Junkies knew better than to cheat him. It was time DU suffered the consequences of crossing him.

The plan formulating in his head went no further than thought. Joe took advantage of his silence and landed a punch to his jaw, knocking Finn back on the bed and stunning him into complacency. "You're more clever than I thought, kid," he spat out, reaching down and grabbing a bag before slinging it over his shoulder. "At first I thought it was about the chick. Some piece of ass you wanted to get a hold of, puttin' on some scheme to be her knight in shining armor. Didn't make sense that you'd even tell Charlie about it. But now I know why you told him and why you threw out that little babysitter idea. You knew

Charlie would send me with you. He'd never let his precious prodigy go off on his own."

Despite's Joe's conviction at his own words, Finn shook his head, one hand rubbing his aching jaw. "I don't know what you're talking about. I'm here to find—"

"Yeah, yeah. Your little girlfriend. It was a good scheme. But I know what's going on up here." Joe lifted a finger and tapped his temple. "The best laid plans go to shit when you tell everyone what you're doing, smartass. I knew I had to knock you out when you confessed who you were really lookin' for, get the truth out of you when you woke up on my terms. Then you made it even easier on me. You should learn to keep your mouth shut when you're sleeping. Then people won't know when you're plottin' behind their backs."

When Finn made to move off the bed, Joe lashed out, his foot connecting with ribs. Finn grunted and fell back. "You shoulda let the past be the past. Would have made my day so much easier."

Refusing to back down, Finn pushed up from the mattress, only to have a gun pressed to the center of his forehead. "Be a good boy and stay there," Joe ordered, his hand steady as it gripped the weapon. "Now, I've got places to be. Loose ends to tie up now that it turns out you ain't as slick as you think you are. 'Ole DU here is gonna take good care of you."

With a knowing grin, Joe stomped out of the room, the door slamming behind him. The sound echoed between the remaining men. Finn's heart pounded sorely as he searched his sides, desperate for a way out, but he couldn't think straight. It was too quiet in his head, the silence scattering his thoughts, save for one.

This would be his end. In this filthy hotel room, looking up at the man he never wanted to see again.

"Just you and me now," DU sneered, cracking his knuckles. "Just like old times."

CHAPTER 18

THE MOTEL ROOM was too small, walls seeming to close in and force the two men together. Finn thought DU would waste no time either killing him or attempting to reenact his favorite filthy pastime. He was surprised when the man simply pulled up a chair and set it in front of the door, then lowered himself into it.

"Sit." The single word was an order, not a suggestion. Finn found his body doing as he was told and hating himself for it. "Good boy."

"Fuck off," Finn growled in response. He wasn't a kid anymore. Nights of silent protests were over.

DU smiled and stretched, palms sliding down the chair arms. "It's been many, many years, hasn't it? I'm sad you never tried to find me."

"Cut the shit. You didn't want to be found."

"Oh? What makes you so sure?"

Finn thought back to the days in his mother's house,

all the hushed conversations he overheard. "Talk around town was you skipped out to Georgia. No one knew where. Or if they did, they weren't talking."

"Smart people," DU mused, shifting in the chair so his legs were spread wider. "Yet here we are now. One might guess you wanted to find me."

Finn's eyes narrowed. "One might think too highly of himself."

Another leery grin. Another raised brow as shifty eyes roved over Finn. "I do enjoy our ... oral foreplay." He winked, the motion curdling in Finn's gut. "I must say, time has been good to you."

"Can't say the same about you."

The smile only widened. "Come now, don't be like that. We had such good times together."

A claw clutched at Finn's insides, gripping him in disgust and humiliation. Why, after all this time, did the man still have such power over him? He didn't understand his own weaknesses. And he sure as hell wasn't willing to talk about them.

As much to defy DU as to piss him off, Finn leapt up from the bed. "I plan on having a real good time tonight, ripping your throat from your body."

The threat brought DU to his feet. He wasn't a large man, but his every move exuded a self-assurance that would send most men to their knees. Finn wasn't most men. He stood his ground, letting DU stalk closer, watching him carefully.

DU stopped an arm's length away. "Such big talk," he said in his low, raspy tone, "for a little boy who cries himself to sleep."

"It's not gonna work," Finn snapped back, refusing to

let his mind take him to that place. "You're right. Time has been good to me. I ain't that kid anymore. You left town, scared of Charlie I always figured, and you missed a whole hell of a lot."

"Did I?" DU's head cocked to the side almost playfully, but the frown tightening his mouth spoke of his growing anger. "I certainly don't recall missing your precious little girl."

That was all Finn needed before he launched into attack. Yes, time had favored him, wrapping his arms in solid muscle and giving him the strength he needed to finally be the one knocking someone to the ground. DU dropped when Finn's fist connected with his jaw, but he was already countering, his shoulder ramming into Finn's gut and sending them both to the floor.

Grappling for control, Finn grunted as he was struck somewhere in the face, his head slamming against the floor. DU's face hovered over him, a contorted mask of rage lined with the love of the fight, the expression tightening when the younger man got a hand around his throat.

"What did you do to her?" Finn asked around a mouthful of blood. He was tempted to spit it in DU's face, but the haunted child inside him feared the consequence of such an action.

DU grinned despite the hand around his throat, thin lips pulling back to reveal yellow teeth. "Oh, boy, you already know the answer to that."

Finn's hand slipped, sending his childhood nightmare down on top of him. The weight was too familiar. Sickeningly familiar.

You should teach your momma how to pay her debts. The man's voice from fifteen years past flooded Finn's mind. *Otherwise good boys with bad mommas have to pay for them.*

How many times had he heard those words? Had there ever been a time when he didn't know what they meant, what it meant would soon happen to him? How loud had he screamed for his mother to make it stop, until he simply stopped crying at all?

He'd been scared as a child. But as Finn glared up at DU now, recognizing the set of the man's jaw, the glint in his watery eyes, the way his hand tapped on his belt buckle, he felt nothing but fury. Not for him. Not for the little boy he once was, the man he never got to become. But for Snow. However she was involved, whatever her father did to owe his debt, however fate intervened to make sure they heard one another's thoughts … his fury had all been leading up to this moment.

"You are done," Finn snarled, finding a strength within himself he never knew he had. Two hands shoved against DU's chest and he rose out from beneath him. "You are done taking payment. Now you owe *me*."

DU laughed, loud and wild and with complete abandon, a laugh accompanied by a storm of fists. Each one found their mark until Finn finally lost his balance and fell, landing hard on his knees, the jolt sending shards of pain through his back. But he didn't have time to react. His body was thrust forward against the bed as DU hit him from behind, wrenching an arm behind his back.

"Don't say you haven't thought about me," the man rasped, shoving up against Finn, whose jaw clenched with disgust. "Don't say you haven't missed me. I know I've certainly missed you."

A hand fisted in Finn's hair, yanking his head back

and exposing his throat. He felt hot breath against his skin, the wet trail of a tongue below his ear. He could have fought, flung himself backward and tackled his opponent, but he didn't. Instead he let DU believe himself the victor, as his hand stealthily lowered to his pocket, where he always kept pieces of wood and metal.

One chance. One shot to end this nightmare once and for all. *Don't fuck it up*, he ordered. *Be a fucking bad-ass.*

Trembling fingers closed over the scrap metal, feeling jagged edges he hadn't yet had a chance to smooth. Retracting his arm and making a fist, Finn gave himself only one second to allow his vision to tunnel, his senses to focus on the body behind him, the feel of breath and tongue and teeth, before he yanked his captured arm free and spun.

The metal buried itself in DU's throat. Blood spurted from the torn-open wound, but Finn didn't stop. With a rage-induced scream covering all the years of his pain, he drove the metal in deeper, not feeling it slice his hand in his fury, spurred on by the gurgling pain erupting from his enemy.

DU fell forward on top of Finn, whose arm shook with the strength to support his weight and shove the scrap steel farther. Beady black eyes stared down at him vacantly, the smallest sparks of life left in them, and thin lips parted to gape for final gasps of air.

Never had Finn been filled with such grim and carnal satisfaction. It strengthened his arm, sending the metal through another layer. "Debts have to be paid," he growled in DU's ear, feeling hot blood sluice down his hand and arm.

Only when the body stopped shuddering did Finn

slide out from under it. For too long a moment all he could do was stare down at DU, thinking back to all the years he'd dreamed of seeing the man bleeding at his feet.

"You took everything from me," he muttered, unable to stop himself from kicking the body before reminding himself he had other places to be. Rushing to the bathroom, he stripped off his soiled shirt and wrapped it in a bag from the trash can, then did his best to wash the blood off his face, neck, and arms using one of the towels by the sink. Water splashed over the counter each time he rinsed the towel, running red down the drain so thick it threatened to stain the cheap porcelain.

"Good enough," he said to himself in the mirror, barely seeing the bruises starting to color his eye and jawline, or his ribs, or the light smears of blood still staining his chest. He threw on his leather jacket, then grabbed his blood-stained shirt and headed for the door, sparing DU one last look almost as an afterthought.

"Maybe you'll be useful after all." Finn paused long enough to dig through DU's pockets for his car keys and grab the gun holstered at the small of his back, momentarily surprised his mother's former dealer didn't try to use it on him, then he was out the door, making sure the scrap of steel was back in his pocket before pulling the locked door shut.

The body would eventually be found. Cops would be called, forensics sent out for testing. Nothing he could do about it now. He had neither the time nor the skills to drag the body to the car, dump it, and somehow strip the room clean of all DNA and fingerprints. At least he had the murder weapon—he could dispose of it later, assuming the cops didn't find him before he had the chance.

As long as he got to Snow first, Finn didn't care what happened to him after.

It made him feel dirty, sitting in the driver's seat of DU's car, despite how pristine the interior appeared to be. DU had always been a neat freak—no matter how revolting his favorite pastimes. His skin felt like it was crawling as Finn started the engine and prepared to peel out, before realizing he had no idea where he was, let alone which direction to go.

A quick pocket check revealed his phone was missing. "Shit," Finn muttered, remembering tossing it to Joe and never getting it back. That had to be intentional. Joe seemed to think there was some big conspiracy against him, which was probably why he'd called DU, for backup.

"And to get rid of me once and for all," he continued his train of thought, reluctantly understanding why Joe had brought DU into it, even if he still didn't know how Snow fit into the equation. Somehow, her father owed a debt to Joe or DU—or maybe even both.

Just how far did Charlie's reach go? And did he know about Snow?

Loose ends. Joe had mentioned getting rid of loose ends. Finn could only imagine what that meant, who he intended to get rid of, but one fact was clear—he had to get to Iron Creek Estates.

"Where the fuck am I?" he mumbled, turning in his seat and peering through the windows at license plates. A handful of Carolinas, and the majority listing Georgia. So Joe really had brought him across the state.

The only problem—he was in the wrong state.

Finn tore out of the parking lot, able to see the highway from the hotel. He'd already merged onto the northbound side when he realized just how far he had to go. All this time he thought Snow was in Georgia, believing the news anchors and police who offered mere best guesses. But she had revealed the truth about her location, and now Joe knew he knew as well.

If he drove fast enough, maybe he could catch up to the man who was now his number one enemy. Catch up to him, and rip his throat out.

The sound of the highway lulled Finn into thought—always one of the best times he'd ever been able to connect to Snow. Maybe it was the rushing of road beneath tires, or the steady passing of trees. Whatever allowed for an easier connection, he welcomed it, and focused on the faint feel of Snow's consciousness within him.

Snow? You still with me?

An ominous quiet permeated the car, rising above the rushing.

Snow? Come on, Snow. Come back to me.

He waited, hands tightening on the wheel, hating the feel of this strange car, hating even more having to smell DU all around him. When this was all over, he was going to torch the fucker. With DU in it, if he had the opportunity.

Finn?

He nearly swerved off the road at the sudden burst of a soft, melodic voice in his head. His breath rushed out in relief. "Snow, thank god," he said aloud, needing to hear her name spoken as though to make her presence that much realer.

I'm coming, Snow. I'm on my way, I swear.

Silence, for too long, before she replied, *Just leave me*.

His brow furrowed. Shifting in the seat, Finn focused on feeling her, honing in on their heightened senses and strange ability to feel the other's life. And when he finally did reach her, he was hit with such a shock of desolation and emptiness it nearly sucked the will to live right out of him.

...Snow? Talk to me. Tell me what happened.

He came ... a debt ... It hurts, Finn. It won't stop.

She sounded drunk, maybe even high, but what scared him most was the resignation in her voice. He didn't need to ask again to know what happened. This feeling of emptiness, a silently screaming wish to let go and break into millions of tiny pieces too small and fragmented to ever hurt again ... It was devastatingly familiar.

And he'd let it happen. He didn't figure it out in time, where she was, who had her. Destiny had given him this gift to hear her thoughts and feel all her wonderful emotions, and he took it for granted, never pushing to discover her true identity and bring her into his safe and protective arms.

Now she was refusing their gift. He could feel her trying to sever the connection, not wanting him to see inside her torture. But he wouldn't let her, not when she needed him most. Some might say she'd only been in captivity a few days, but he knew there was no such thing as *only* when it came to her abductors. There was constant, unrelenting, unforgiving pain, and the knowledge that the future would hold only shameful memories.

Snow, I know it hurts and I know you're scared, but

you have to hold on for me, okay? His tone was full of fear, threatening to break even in thought.

It seemed ten miles passed before she replied, *Why? ... What's there to hold on to?*

Me, was his immediate answer. *Hold on to me, Snow. Our friendship. Hold on to us.*

I don't ... want a life like this.

"Stop it," Finn whispered, a plea to whatever god might be listening to take away her hurt and let her be in peace. She was too good, too kind. "Make it happen to me. Not her."

But to Snow he said, *You have to fight. You have to be brave.*

He heard a sigh in his mind, felt the indifference of a girl giving up. *Sometimes being brave means letting go ... even when that's the hardest thing to do.*

That's bullshit and you know it. His response was clipped and tinged with fear. Part of him hoped his hastily snapped reply would break her out of the fog, but deep down he knew that wasn't the way to reach her. So, he tried again. *Snow, pain goes away, okay? You have to fight. Fight for me. Don't give up on me.*

It hurts. She was whimpering now, tears lacing her words. *I don't want to live through this.*

"Goddamn it, Snow, don't do this to me!" He shouted the words at the same time he thought them. Foot pressing harder, he floored it down the highway, his only thought now on getting to Iron Creek Estates.

She heard his demand, the urgency in his voice, the fear he held that she wouldn't be there when he finally arrived. But, she didn't care. Her new reality was too overwhelming.

Her mouth and nose were crusted over with dried blood, bottom lip and jaw so enflamed she could barely open her mouth. She suspected her nose was broken, and maybe her cheekbone, judging by the stabs of pain radiating down the right side of her face. One eye was swollen shut, the other blurry. Snow didn't remember what happened to them. There were so many punches and slaps, and a belt, with a cold metal buckle … She stopped counting after the first thirty strikes.

Her back felt like it was burning, the fire starting from a hole in her shoulder made from a cigar pressed against bare skin. All over her skin the pain crawled, sliding into her ribs, hammering into her forehead, cramping in her hands and toes as she shivered.

And she was hungry. So hungry. Her captors hadn't given her anything to eat or drink, let alone anywhere to wash herself. For who knew how many days she lay in her own blood and sweat and filth. The shame of it all ripped her soul apart.

And then there was Finn, asking what they did to her. Unspeakable things. Things she couldn't say, would never be able to say. Not out loud, not in her head to her best friend. She would never stop feeling them. There was no escape from the horrors this room had seen.

Snow, pain goes away, okay?

"It will never go away," she whispered, curling into a ball on her side and wincing at the red-hot poker jabbing in her ribs. Her back prickled with goosebumps where her shirt was torn and hanging down one shoulder.

Fight for me.

"I'm too tired to fight." The words were spoken into bare legs as she buried her head in her knees. The floor beneath her reeked of sin and shame.

Don't give up on me.

It hurt. Everywhere, outside, inside. Nothing could heal these scars. *I don't want to live through this.* She wasn't sure if the words were spoken or thought, and decided she didn't care. Snow meant what she said. There was no chance of going back. Even if Finn did save her, how could she return home knowing this was her father's fault? Worse, having no idea what he'd done to owe a debt, but knowing he didn't try to save her? And how could she go back to her life remembering what had been done to her?

Finn's voice jolted her back to the present. *Goddamn it, Snow, don't do this to me!*

It was already done.

CHAPTER 19

H E COULDN'T HEAR her anymore. The buzz of Snow's voice even when not speaking had gone too quiet, spurring Finn to drive faster, pushing his body to its limits. Snatches of sleep in gas station parking lots preceded energy drink chugs and fast food. Speed limits were mere guidelines, eyes on the lookout for cops. And only when his body absolutely demanded it did he go against better judgment and give in to sleep.

And yet, still he felt he was always one step behind Joe.

The road stretched out before him, one long tunnel of asphalt and trees. In the dead of night, everything blurred together as the world became awash in white spots and black shadow, surrounding the stolen car in a black wave threatening to suck him under.

"Keep it together," Finn ordered himself, wiping a hand down his face and shaking his head. Grabbing another energy drink from the passenger seat, he gulped it down in a few long swallows. The can joined the others on the floorboard in the backseat. The fabricated energy buzzed through him—the crash would come, but only when he allowed it.

At some point night faded into dawn and Finn found himself squinting into a brilliant orange sun. It lit the path before him, guiding him until he saw the sign for his exit just a few miles up the road. His foot pressed harder, tires barely gaining traction as he sped off the highway and finally down a local road.

He could feel her, a palpable string drawing him forward. Even in dawn's early light he saw his surroundings crystal clear, led forward by fate's cold hand connecting him to Snow's resting place. The map formed in his mind effortlessly; he didn't question it, following the route predetermined for him.

And then he saw it, the faded yellow sign with *Iron Creek Estates* sprawled in swirling black letters above a picture of a river winding through the forest. A pretty picture masking the darkness within. Finn eyed the sign as he entered the neighborhood, hating it and everything it stood for, before searching for his Mustang.

It didn't take long to find. Joe wasn't hiding—not that he had to. Not here, not anymore.

Finn all but skidded into the driveway, leaving the car at an angle as he scoped out the scene. The street was quiet in the early morning, mobile homes spaced out on plots of land marked by broken-down vehicles and wood-post fences. All seemed at peace, but Finn knew what lurked on the other side of drawn curtains—neighbors who saw everything, even if they kept it all to themselves.

Gun in hand, Finn slid out of the car, not bothering to shut the door. He didn't care if everyone knew he was just outside or if anyone stole the vehicle. There was only one person his list, and no one would stand in his way. His mind raced with one word—*Joe*—as heavy footsteps pounded up the cracked-paver walk, atop three rickety stairs.

The door to the trailer was shut, but only for a second before Finn's foot connected with the handle, cracking the entire frame as the door flew open, slamming into the wall with a resounding crash. He stomped inside, the odor of sweat and mold filling his nostrils—and the hint of something else. An underlying copper stench that could only be attributed to one thing.

One foot crossed the threshold, then another, his body slipping inside and sliding against the wall as he edged his way along. Not a sound was heard save for his own quiet breaths and beating heart. But he knew they were in there. He could feel another body, living, breathing.

Waiting.

Finn rounded the corner, gun aimed at nothing but ready. He wouldn't think about the fact that he didn't really know how to use it, about how foreign DU's revolver felt in his hand—he was used to Charlie's Berettas, and even rifles—about how he'd never actually had to fire a weapon. What mattered was he found the person the bullet was meant for.

He saw the edge a kitchen cabinet, yellow wood splattered with red. Bile rising in his throat, Finn tightened his grip on the gun and advanced, stumbling when he took just two steps and caught sight of the object laying across the entrance to the kitchen.

His eyes narrowed as he focused on what he was see-ing. They widened when he realized what it was—a hand, leading to a body he couldn't see on the other side of the wall. Sucking in a breath, Finn rounded the corner, ready to attack and let loose a flurry of bullets, but the room, a filthy kitchen cluttered with dirty dishes, was empty.

Except for the woman lying lifeless on the floor.

A quick scout of the room confirmed it was clear. Finn shuffled in, stepping carefully around the body. It wasn't Snow. He couldn't see her face, but still he knew; he could feel it. Kneeling, Finn pushed the woman onto her back and took in her face. She was older, gaunt and cold, with matted hair and bloodshot eyes staring vacantly at the ceiling. A wound slashed across her throat seeped blood.

He hoped her death had been quick and painless, something she never saw coming. It surprised him to feel such mercy—and blamed it on this being the first mur-dered woman he'd ever seen. Not his first dead body, there were plenty of junkie overdoses over the years, but none of them ever had their throats split wide open.

"Loose ends."

Joe's voice from the doorway had Finn looking up slowly, gun at the ready. The older, far stronger man was leaning against frame, arms crossed, stance too casual for the crime splayed out before him. Finn didn't see a gun or knife on him, but knew there had to be one or both tucked away somewhere.

The body was a buffer between them. Blood slowly spread from beneath the woman, toward Finn's boot-clad feet. He took a step back before asking, "Why her?"

Joe spared the woman a passing glance. "She knew

too much."

"Did…" The words stuck in his throat; he forced them out. "Did Charlie order this? Did he order you to take Snow?"

"Charlie?" Joe chuckled and shook his head. "Charlie is an old fuckin' man who ain't got it in him to rule anymore. I'm done following Charlie's orders."

"Then … why?"

"Why?" Pushing off the doorway, Joe straightened to his full height, his glare bearing down on the younger boy with the weight of many years' pain. "Only four people know what went down that night. Since you're here, I can only assume 'ole DU is out of the equation. I'd be impressed if I actually liked you, kid." His eyes narrowed, looking down at the woman before returning to Finn. "This broad here cuts down the witnesses to two. That leaves me and you."

One hand reached behind his back. Finn saw the motion and sprang, lunging for Joe before a weapon could be drawn. He could have used his own gun, but the fury within craved blood. Finn wanted to make the man suffer for what he'd done, to tear him apart with bare hands.

One punch landed solidly across Joe's cheek, another to his chin. It was like hitting a wall, each strike sending spikes of pain through Finn's hand while barely slowing his rival, who matched each hit with his own. Stars exploded in front of Finn's eyes when a fist was swiped across his temple. His vision dulled and he dropped to his knees, the momentary falter all Joe needed to take control.

"All this time I thought you never knew," Joe rasped as he dragged a half-conscious Finn from the kitchen, down the hall, into the bedroom at the end. Blood was smeared around his lips, coating his teeth. "DU had her first, 'til I took that sweet young thing all for myself."

"Fucking son of a bitch," Finn snarled, grabbing at the hand fisted in his hair but not able to free himself. He'd lost his gun somewhere in the kitchen. Twisting against the hold, he frantically searched for Joe's, not seeing it anywhere.

"All this time I thought you never knew," Joe continued as though he wasn't dragging another person along the floor. "Had my mask on and everything. You did good, you little shit. Barging in to Charlie's office that day, demandin' a job. Playin' the part of wannabe thug all them years. Actin' like some hero off to save a girl. And I played right into it, didn't I?"

Finn grunted when he was tossed to the floor but immediately picked himself up, refusing to show weakness. He was a bad-ass, not some weakling victim Joe could toss around like a ragdoll. "Played into what?" he asked around a mouthful of blood, entirely confused by the man's ranting.

"Don't play dumb with me, kid."

"You don't play dumb with me," Finn shot back, ready to lunge. "What the fuck are you talking about?"

"I didn't catch on until your little sleep-talkin' fuckup." Joe laughed to himself, an incredulous and insane sound. "You're smarter than I gave you credit for."

He was done with this idiotic tirade. "I don't give a shit what you think is happening here. I don't even care why you brought Snow into it. Just tell me where she is. What did you do with her?"

It struck him then, where he was, the stench in the room, the reason why Joe brought him here instead of killing him in the kitchen. Slowly, almost unwillingly, his eyes moved to the closet. The door was shut, black shadows creeping out from the cracks and crawling toward him, beckoning him forward.

Before he could move, Joe was on him. Finn was propelled backward into the wall but caught himself, bracing his back against the window and landing a solid hit to Joe's gut. His opponent doubled over, giving Finn the opportunity to send a fist into his jaw, another to his cheekbone.

Hit for hit they matched one another, tumbling over the bed in a flood of fists and blood. Finn wasn't a particularly skilled fighter and his strength would never match Joe's, but his blood burned with a wrath he'd never known before, blinding him in a red haze.

All around them cheap paneling splintered. Glass shattered and clothing was torn, blood bursting from lips and noses. No words were spoken, only furious shouts and pained grunts. Finn managed a tight headlock, sending his fist into Joe's gut, but the hold didn't last. His opponent spun from his grasp and countered, sending Finn flying against the wall with a sharp kick to the back.

There was no time to push off, no chance to retaliate. Finn felt his body tugged away from the wall mere seconds before he was thrown to the floor. Exhaustion racked his limbs, weakening his attempts to shove the stronger man off.

Cold fingers wrapped around Finn's throat. Joe's hands tightened, his weight pinning Finn to the floor. "Your momma done finally confessed, huh?" he asked in a tone that was too calm compared to his maniacal laughter earlier. "She musta really hated you, you little punk. She knew the consequences of opening her whore mouth."

"Fuck you," Finn spat back, his voice rough and gar-bled. Blood dripped down his throat, choking him as much as the hand gripping his neck.

"Ain't so tough now, are you? I shoulda ended you a long time ago. You wanna know why I let you live?" Joe's face lowered until it was mere inches from Finn's. "'Cause I thought, even if you did know the truth, me and 'ole DU fucked you up so much you knew better than to open that bratty fucking mouth of yours."

Breath wheezed out of Finn's closing throat, black spots dancing before his eyes. Still, he felt the rage build-ing at the admission and managed to say, "I never ... for-got ... what you did to me."

Joe chuckled, a harsh, unforgiving sound. He ground Finn's head farther into the floor and laughed again at his wince. "You always were 'ole DU's favorite. Skinny little kid that shook like a leaf whenever someone looked at him. You were the perfect toy. But he liked your girl too. We both did." Now the smile faded, replaced by an ex-pression far more sinister. "You still wanna know what we did to her?"

He didn't want to listen. He didn't want to hear the truth. But what he wanted no longer mattered.

"I broke every finger and every toe, one by one." Per-verse pleasure glinted in Joe's eyes. "I remember it so clearly. All the cracks. They were like music. And her skin." He rolled his shoulders as though gratified by the thought, his body responding to the jerks of the boy be-neath him as he kicked his feet, struggling for freedom. "So soft and slick. So easy to cut open. And every time she screamed, it just made me want to do it all again."

An unnatural sound escaped Finn, a guttural scream filled with years of hate. It would be his last breath, the air fleeing his lungs, unable to draw in more, but he released it willingly even against the burn in his chest. His hands released Joe's wrists and clutched the sides of his face, thumbs digging into dark eyes. Joe arched back, trying to shake off Finn's grip, but he held strong, ready to die if it meant taking this fucker down with him.

A sharp shout sounded from Joe's lips to match the blood starting to drip down his face, but he too had made his vow. Finn's airway closed and the fight left his arms, and he peered up at Joe through spotted vision to see the face of death above him, contorted into carnal satisfaction.

I'm ... sorry ... Snow.

His last thought would be of her, the girl who made his life worth living. He would see her face, hear her voice, imagine them together in another world, finally united.

But the vision he struggled to see never came. Instead his fading blue eyes locked on that sick pleasure in the narrowed orbs above him, watching as it erupted into panic for only a second before being replaced by emptiness. Blood and brain splattered Finn's face. The hands around his throat loosened, Joe's body falling on top of his, jerking with its final moments of life.

Air returned to his lungs in sputtering gasps. Each breath burned as it entered, momentarily distracting Finn from the dead man crushing him, the revolting odor of a skull turned inside out. It was the smell that finally broke his daze and he shoved at the body, scrambling to his knees while spinning around to the door, shocked to see Charlie standing there with his arm still raised, gun pointed at Joe. Next to him stood Chix, Infinity's most-feared bouncer, the same bouncer who'd granted Finn entry as a kid in need of a job.

Finn didn't know how Charlie got there, or why he was there. Nor did he care. Questions could be asked later; right now he had to get to the closet. The crawl to the other side of the room seemed to take hours, though it was likely less than a minute before his hand touched the peeling wood. His fingers trembled.

Snow was in there. He could feel her presence, except this time in a different way, a way that told him he was forever alone in the world. But he had to know, and so Finn pushed open the closet door, tears pricking the corners of his eyes, unable to wash away the sight of his failure.

CHAPTER 20

A YOUNG GIRL lay upon the cold carpet, knees drawn up to her chest, hands mangled, open lesions on her bare back. Yellow-gold hair was spread around her head in a halo. It seemed she was sleeping, her expression hauntingly calm. If not for the abuse her body had gone through, she would be just a girl playing hide-and-seek in the closet.

Except she was still, so still. *Why won't she move?* Finn asked himself. He refused to believe she was gone. Not his Snow. Tentatively, Finn reached out to touch her, to insist she wake and tell him she was okay.

But she didn't respond. The girl lay motionless, blood smudged along dirt and bruise-covered legs, arms, jawline, throat. Everywhere. She was hurt everywhere, and Finn could do nothing but lower himself to the floor next to her.

"Don't leave me," he whispered, needing to talk to her, to feel her. His hand touched her cheek, feeling cold flesh beneath his fingertips, then moved to her hair, feeling the soft curls marred by dried blood.

But she didn't respond.

He moved closer, hoping, praying, deluding himself into believing his warmth would thaw the ice coating her skin. His arms wrapped around her and he began to rock, the steady back and forth a bitter balm to his aching heart. Whatever tough-guy persona he'd tried to put on earlier— tried to put on his entire life—melted away and, for the first time since he was seven years old, Finn let himself cry.

And, still, she didn't respond.

What was the point, he asked a cruel world that didn't care. What was the point of hearing Snow's thoughts, of fate bringing together two kids who needed a friend, just to tear them apart? Or maybe it wasn't the world that was at fault. Maybe *he* was to blame. Because of who he was. Because he didn't try hard enough. Because he was mean where she was sweet, tough where she was soft.

A hand touched his shoulder, startling Finn out of his misery. The effort it took to lift his head exhausted the boy. Charlie stood over him, an expression of rage tinted with grief coloring his aged face. He looked so much older in this moment, Finn noted.

"We need to leave."

Finn shrugged off his hand, but Charlie's grip only tightened. "I'm not leaving her. I'm not failing her. Not again."

"I'm not giving you a choice." Over his shoulder, Charlie said to the bouncer still standing just outside the door, "Call the cleanup crew. Get rid of this mess and the one at the hotel Joe was tracked to. You know what to do if there are any witnesses. I'll take care of the rest."

Finn heard the order, but couldn't process it. Once he would have been terrified by Charlie's tone, all business with no room for negotiation, a deadly reminder of everything the man was capable of. Now he didn't care what followed the man's demands.

"You did this," Finn accused, one hand gently brushing the soft yellow of Snow's hair. In some part of his mind he knew it was irrational—Joe and DU were their own brand of psycho, their boss never being one for kidnapping and torture—but it helped to blame someone other than himself.

Behind him, Charlie cleared his throat. "Yes, I suppose in some way I did."

The admission did little to comfort the young man kneeling in the closet. Nor did the tug on his shoulder suggesting he move from his cramped spot.

"Get off me!" Finn shouted as Charlie attempted to haul him out of the closet. Charlie sighed, the sound both annoyed and saddened, but it went ignored. The young man at his feet remained focused on his rocking, on the quiet mumbling beneath his breath speaking of his failure, his inability to protect the only girl he ever loved.

In his devastation, he didn't hear Charlie mutter, "This is for your own good." In senses overtaken by the emptiness Snow's absence left behind, he didn't feel the bite of pain as a needle slid into his neck. When he slumped over, the drug working its way through his system, Finn could only find happiness in the hope that, maybe, he was finally going home with Snow.

He dreamt of cramped closets and cold winter nights.

Flashes of childhood nightmares burst against the backs of his closed eyes—his mother slapping him for no reason at all, his stomach growling after three days of no food, hulking figures creeping into his room in the middle of the night reminding him it was time to pay his mother's debt ... mornings after when she pretended not to notice the bruises and tears.

We don't ask for help, she'd always told him. Don't ask for help. Don't be a child. Don't cry or show weakness or let people see you in need.

We are better than that. Better than what, he'd always wondered. Better than the kids at school who always had lunches? Better than the rich people who didn't have to lie and cheat to get their money?

You got that, you little shit? He got it, all right. Never ask for help. Be better than everyone else. And watch as your best friend dies because of it.

Snow asked for help, he told himself in sleep. And he let her down.

When Finn finally opened his eyes, they were wet with unshed tears. Echoes of Snow's screams for help sounded in his ears, out of tune with the birds chirping outside the window across from his bed. Finn blinked against the harsh sun, instantly annoyed that he was once again waking up with no idea how he got there. He'd always thought himself to be smarter, tougher, than that.

Searching the room with a quick turn of his aching head, he realized quickly he was home in his apartment. The feel of his bed was familiar, though not welcome. He shouldn't be this comfortable.

Finn's brow furrowed as he continued his roaming

gaze—the fish tank he usually forgot to clean, clothes strewn across the floor—until finally landing on Charlie sitting in a chair in the corner. His boss was awake and staring right at him with those ice-blue eyes that could cut through even the strongest of men. Except now, they looked tired, even as his rigid stance suggested dominance, his face having aged considerably in the past week. It was unnerving to see the usually suave businessman looking so out of sorts.

Movement at the door caught Finn's attention. He looked over to see Chix standing against the wall, hands clasped in front of him, position ready to leap into action. For what, Finn wasn't sure. Images of Charlie holding a gun, murder set in his expression, Chix at his side with his own weapon at the ready, returned to Finn's mind. The trailer. Joe trying to kill him. DU bleeding out in a motel room.

"What…" Finn's voice came out rough and garbled. He touched a hand to his throat, wincing at the tender flesh. If his boss noticed, he didn't provide any indication of sympathy or concern. "What happened to Joe? To … DU?"

"They're gone," Charlie said simply. Finn turned his head slightly, seeing the meaning behind the statement in his eyes. He knew what "gone" meant. When Charlie wanted someone gone, he said the word and the person disappeared as though they never existed at all. If he said Joe and DU were gone, then it meant more than their deaths. All traces of their existence were wiped out. Finn didn't care to wonder what resources Charlie had at his disposal for such a feat. It was enough to know they were gone.

"What about ... what about Annette?"

"Given a proper burial." Now there was regret replacing stone-cold killer. "But also gone."

Swallowing back bitter bile in his throat, Finn dreaded his next question. "...Where is Snow?" When Charlie merely stared down at him, he tried again. "Don't ... don't tell me she's gone." Again he received no response. His blood began to boil, the wordless reply fueling his body. Just as he made to move off the bed, Charlie motioned with one hand to the bouncer, who Finn realized wasn't protecting from anyone getting in, but, rather, from him getting out.

The bedroom door opened slowly. A man and woman in white lab coats entered, holding what looked like an old-fashioned doctor's bag. Finn knew what was coming and raged against it. He lifted his tired and aching body from the bed but Chix was there, one beefy hand pressed against his chest. Charlie rose as well, too calm as he approached.

"Don't fucking tell me she's gone!" Finn shouted at him, desperately trying to remove Chix's hand and failing miserably. "Don't you tell me she's fucking *gone*, Charlie!"

"I won't tell you she's gone," Charlie replied smoothly, sounding like he was talking to a child.

"Then tell me where she is!" His demand echoed through the room, down the hall, matched by the doctor's curt order to the nurse just inside the room. "What did you do with her? What did you do to me? And what the hell are you doing here?"

The man at his bedside tried to calm him, pressing a firm hand to his shoulder. "Relax. We are trying to help you."

"Like hell you are! Where is Snow?"

The nurse rushed to the doctor's side, handing him something from the leather bag in her hand. As Chix continued to restrain their patient, the doctor continued to prepare a sedative, seemingly oblivious to the struggle taking place mere inches from him. Seeing the needle sent Finn into another bout of rage, strength fueling his limbs as he shot up from the bed, only to be thrown back down by a muscled arm. Wild blue eyes traced that arm, his grief and exhaustion-drugged brain filtering through faces until it landed on Joe's, a hallucination as much as a memory securing him to the mattress as the nurse approached cautiously.

"You son of a bitch," Finn growled, coming to the only conclusion that made sense. "You knew about her all along, didn't you? You got rid of her because I was getting too good. Her father had nothing to do with it, did he? You goddamn *liar*!"

"Relax," Charlie said again, his tone firm but his eyes filled with gloom. "You're speaking nonsense and you know it. This is for your own good."

"The fuck it is." Finn struggled, but felt the needle pierce his skin and was powerless against its effects. A painful warmth sliced through him and took the fight out of his body. He slumped against the mattress. "Where..." His voice was weak, punctuated by a sob. "Where is Snow?"

The old man swallowed hard, letting one hand drift through Finn's hair. "Tommy, Snow is ... Snow is dead."

CHAPTER
21

THE STEADY HUM of a corner fish tank filled the large bedroom. A wide window along the far wall let in thin streams of morning sunlight through the clouds, lighting up the grayish-blue walls and carpeted floors. And there, in the center of the room, lay a boy not much older than twenty, his grandfather sleeping soundly next to him.

The door opened and closed with a small click, stirring the man with deep worry lines etched around ice-blue eyes. He peered across the room at the middle-aged woman who had entered, her expression gentle and friendly. Standing, he ran his hands down his dress shirt, smoothing out the wrinkles before straightening to assume his usual air of grandeur.

"Dr. Jenn," he greeted coolly, though she could hear the underlying tone of concern. "Please, excuse my state. Thank you for coming."

The doctor nodded, her fiery-red hair framing her face in soft curls. She accepted his proffered hand, then sat in the chair he placed next to the bed, her soft yellow dress swishing around her ankles. "Of course, Charles. You know how much I care for him."

"Yes, well, I don't know how much you can do for him this time. Circumstances have changed."

Another nod, her lips pursed thoughtfully as she looked around the familiar room, then down at Finn. "How long as he been out?"

The man known to most around town as Charles Stone resumed his seat. "A little over two days. He's been sedated twice. Each time he comes out of it, he panics and flies into a rage. We have been sedating him at home. I'm sure you understand why we cannot bring him to a hospital."

The warning was clear, and unnecessary. She did know, and respected those reasons as much as she feared the repercussions of going against them. Instead of replying, Dr. Jenn took a moment to look over the sleeping patient, eyes narrowing thoughtfully when she saw the figurine on the bedside table.

Picking it up, she ran her fingers over the tiny wooden child wearing a painted cape like a superhero, memories taking her back to a time when she marveled over a little boy's ability to create such trinkets. "What's this?"

"One of his figures he left on my front porch." Charles reached into his pocket and pulled out a second figurine, a girl crafted of thin wingnuts and copper wire with yellow-twine hair. Though he didn't give it to the doctor, he did allow her to observe it before securing it away again. "This one was in his pocket when they found him."

"He still makes them? After so many years? So many of our sessions?"

"He never stopped."

The confirmation had Dr. Jenn's eyes lifting from figure to father. "Charles, what happened?"

"You are a respectable doctor, Jennifer, intelligent and knowing. Certainly you saw this coming."

She suspected the reply was a delay rather than an accusation. So, she asked again, "Saw what coming, Charles?"

"His eventual break."

"You know these things can't be predicted, Charles. Especially in his situation." Dr. Jenn folded her hands together. "Now, tell me what happened."

"I thought he was getting better," Charles replied, scrubbing a hand down his face, the tough-man façade fading for only a moment in the presence of an old family friend who he knew could be trusted. "He went out, had fun like a normal teenage boy. Even got himself a girl, a pretty one too. He brought her around a few times, though never to his apartment out back. Only to the main house, the room he had growing up. I didn't know he was still talking to Snow until a week ago, when he said a friend was in trouble and he had to help her. At first I thought…"

His voice faded, prompting the doctor to reach across the bed and touch his hand. "What happened a week ago?"

A deep breath preceded the quiet reply. "My wife … his grandmother, passed away from a heart attack. I'm surprised you hadn't heard."

"I did hear, when I got back in town two days ago," she confessed, eyes downcast. "And I am so sorry for your loss. She was such a lovely woman."

Not wanting to get lost in his own grief, Charles continued. "Her death … it broke what was left of the Tommy we used to know. You know how he was before. Alert, intelligent, not quite sane but still able to live in the world. After I called him with news of my wife's death, it was as though Tommy lost what little grasp he had on the world. It happened so fast, a flip of some kind of mental switch. He no longer recognized me as his grandfather and boss. I was … Well, to be honest, I don't know who he saw me as."

"How do you know he didn't recognize you?"

"When my wife had her heart attack, Tommy was at a party. I called him and ordered him to come to the hospital. Except he never came. He ended up at his apartment out back, and when I confronted him the next morning, he seemed to have no recollection of our conversation the night before. Instead he was rambling about needing time off in order to help a friend. He wouldn't tell me who, but I suspected it was Snow, given how he spoke of her."

Charles shook his head. "He left Infinity and I went home to take care of matters regarding my late wife. Imagine my surprise when someone called me, a young man named Finn who needed a favor, for me to take care of Tommy."

At Dr. Jenn's confused frown, he continued, "That was my reaction as well. He insisted I take care of his little brother, Tommy, while he went to take care of something. I realized then that he was gone. One hour he recognizes me as his boss, in charge of Infinity and all it entails, and the next hour I am a stranger he met when he was eleven years old, trying to track him down at his mother's trailer after he slipped out of the house. And now I was being asked to take care of a little boy who didn't even exist … some other child made up in his mind to make up for the past. All I could do was ensure his safety as he did whatever he had to do to process his grandmother's death, send my most trusted second hand with him for security. And still I failed even at that."

Dr. Jenn's head cocked to the side, trying to process the meaning in his declaration. He didn't give her the opportunity to question him. "There is brilliance in insanity, wouldn't you say, Jennifer? Even when Tommy was lost to the world, some part of him was conscious enough to merge his fantasy into reality. He's the one who suggested I send someone along with him, knowing I would have chosen Joe, the only person who could have possibly known Duane's location after he fled town. A brilliant plan, masked by insanity. I doubt even he knew how perfect he became in his vengeance."

While she didn't understand everything Charles said, the doctor's heart clutched despite the malice hidden in the quiet rambling. It seemed to do the same to the man opposite her, and they both fell quiet, reflecting on the many years shared between them.

The first time she met Tommy he'd been watching an animated film about superhero action figures. At first he'd opened up about his imaginary friend named Snow, excited someone finally believed in her too, but he shut down quickly.

The last time she visited, he'd been a teenager who looked at her like she had three heads for even suggesting he talked to someone in his mind. She still remembered the day so clearly, watching him build a snowman in the backyard with a black-haired girl who achieved the rare feat of making him laugh. Tommy had always loved the winter, spending hours among the white fluff, as both child and adult.

"You always cared so much for him," she commented, perhaps only to break the silence. Just as Dr. Jenn remembered her sessions with Tommy, she also remembered how closely Charles watched. "It always struck me as oddly comforting."

"In what way?"

Her gaze lifted to his, bright eyes twinkling with a knowing glint. "Charles, they call you Top Pop for a reason. I may be a respectable doctor, as you so noted, but our families have always been close. We both know what rumors I hear, and which ones I know are fact."

Charles regarded her with a cautious stare, fingertips tapping together. "Top Pop," he murmured. "Such a ridiculous name. I would love to find the person who came up with it. Those who ever directed it toward me in conversation learned to never do so again."

She smiled despite the underlying meaning to his words. Charles was an old man, but powerful—perhaps the most powerful in the state. His profession was no secret, a successful import and export company masking the trade of narcotics and other illegal products and services. It was a reputation he wore with pride. But Dr. Jenn knew what he kept hidden, the guilt he lived with each day, and the love he felt for a grandson with a tormented soul.

"So, what are your thoughts on how to move forward?"

"I'd like to speak with him when he's awake before making that decision." Conversation now focused once more on the medical, Dr. Jenn pushed back thoughts of less-than-honorable trades and intentions. "My hope is that we can get Tommy back to where he was, get him to properly grieve his grandmother, but if he's truly lost to the state you have described, we may have to take more drastic measures."

"I will not have him committed, Jennifer. You know this."

She held up a hand in gentle defense. "I know. I simply mean a different route. Continued therapy. Medication, perhaps. We can—"

Her suggestion was interrupted by a knock at the door. When Charles made no motion to move, she answered it for him, finding a young woman on the other side, jet-black hair pulled back into a loose bun, shadows under her eyes. "Hello, dear. I assume you're here to see Tommy?"

The girl nodded. Dark eyes roved over the bed, the room, before she replied, "Um … yes. I heard he was home and that he was … injured. Chix let me in."

Now Charles did stand, arms clasped behind his back as he looked over at the young woman and greeted, "Hello, Amelia."

CHAPTER 22

SITTING IN THE soft chair Charles had vacated, Amelia stared down at Tommy, one hand reaching out to stroke his cheek. He looked so peaceful in sleep, so unlike the tough and tormented boy she had known nearly all her life. She'd thought he left her. Found another girl in his mysterious apartment he never took her to, wanted to start a new life with her. Now, seeing him so clearly hurting even while sleeping, part of her wished that had been true.

"He just disappeared," she whispered to whoever was listening. "He seemed a little off lately, but I thought he was just stressed. I don't understand what happened to him." Now she looked over at Charles, who was watching her carefully. "What's wrong with Tommy?"

Instead of answering, Charles gestured to the doctor, who nodded. "Right. I'll take my leave for the day." Dr. Jenn gathered her purse, then pressed a kiss to her fingers and gently touched them to Finn's cheek. "Charles, please let me know when you need me to return."

When she had gone, the older man turned to Amelia, holding an arm toward the door. "Come."

Though it took every bit of nerve she had to defy the man who terrified everyone in town, the young woman shook her head and gripped Finn's hand. "No. Not until you tell me what's going on."

"I'm not going to tell you," Charles said with a hint of irritation. "I'm going to show you. It's time you knew the truth."

AT FIRST, SHE thought Charles was leading her outside to get rid of her, to stop her from seeing or talking to Tommy for some reason. But when he brought her through the porch and into the sprawling two-acre backyard, past a gorgeous stone wall rising high above her head, to an expansive section surrounded by towering oak trees, she realized he was answering her question the only way he could.

Charles stayed at the entrance to the small slice of land tucked away from the rest of the yard, hands in his pockets, as Amelia ventured inside. For a moment she, too, stood on the other side of the wall, not able to comprehend what she saw awaiting her on the other side. But the sight lured her forward, her hands grazing the smooth stone-walled entrance, feeling like she was walking into a fantasy world she'd only ever seen in movies. Her brow furrowed deeper every time she turned her head.

An entire city lay sprawled out before her, miniature in form but no less in grandeur. At her feet began a long road made of tiny scrap-metal cobblestones, winding its way through trees and mountains carved of wood and painted to depict a beautiful fall season filled with brilliant oranges and reds. High up, the mountains were dusted in snow, tiny snowmen lining the hills and valleys.

Her eyes followed the road as her feet stepped carefully along an obvious path. Along the road were vehicles of all different colors constructed of wires and thin strips of steel, some with tiny figures made of what looked like paperclips in the driver and passenger seats. A highway arched over the main path, dipping through the trees before disappearing beyond the boundaries of the wall. Branching off the road were smaller streets leading to stores and neighborhoods, some protected by trees, others by metal gates.

The road wound up, through a grass woodland where wildflowers made trees, into a new tier of the city, where grand homes were built against a forest backdrop. Each house was crafted with a careful hand and close eye for attention, with square and oval windows cut into wooden walls, roofs etched to look like shingles, even huge yards spotted with colorful landscaping. She recognized the home she was in, a black toy Mustang in the driveway.

On the other side of the makeshift city lay another house she recognized, a bright-green trailer sitting on top of a mostly dirt plot of land. It was surrounded by other mobile homes, some of which had children in the yards with tiny basketballs and wire-made bicycles. Farther down the road, all the way at the end and around the corner, a small cemetery was spread out with tiny stone grave markers surrounding a garden. The same cemetery where Amelia found Tommy hiding in all those years ago, the day after … Just, the day after.

This was her town, his town, except … different.

Lights strung throughout the yard's many trees and high-reaching plum pines glistened above the town, illuminating the homes in a soft yellow glow accented by twinkling white, blue, and pink stars high in the sky. A rainbowed prism reflected off the metal roofs, cars, people. Amelia followed the kaleidoscope of color until her eyes settled on a child's tiara with big plastic gemstones tucked up above the mountains. Before she could ponder its meaning, chrome-colored chimes hooked along branches swished together in the cool breeze, their songs bringing the small town alive with music and color.

Amelia's breath caught as she listened to the music, almost able to imagine the town bursting with laughter, children playing, traffic, even gunshots from the parts of the city awash in carefully constructed shadows. The song surrounded her, spinning her in a circle in the middle of the town she'd known her entire life, bringing a smile to her face despite the strange history of this hidden creation.

It was beautiful. Evocative and melancholy and astounding all at once in its glittering existence.

She didn't know how long she stood there, observing the city within a backyard, before she finally found her voice. "I … I don't know what to say about this place. I don't understand." Looking over her shoulder, she saw Charles watching her carefully, unable to read his expression. In this moment he didn't seem like the dangerous gangster everyone said he was, who she knew him to be. "Did … did Tommy create this?"

Eyes on the town, Charles replied, "Created … creating." At her frown, he continued on a sigh, "He has been creating this town since he was seven years old, the day he came to live with us. This is where he lives."

Heart breaking, Amelia whispered with tears in her eyes, "In Silver City."

They sat at a glass table on the patio, the beautiful city of wood and metal creating a colorful backdrop in the distance. On placemats before them were two mugs of tea, though neither one was yet to be touched. Amelia waited, somewhat impatiently, for the elderly man to reveal the secrets of the hidden town.

"Know that what I am about to tell you, I do so only because I believe you may be Tommy's last link to reality," Charles began. The implication to his opening was clear—she was not a member of his trusted circle, and she better keep her mouth shut if she knew what was good for her. Amelia nodded.

"Tommy came to live with us when he was seven. Child Protective Services took him away, and so we took him in. You know this. I would wager most people in this town know. What you never knew was that I didn't want to care for a child, not after what our daughter became, but I would not stand to have my own blood stripped from my family. We knew right away Tommy was sick. My wife hoped we could help him. She tried hard to save him from what he'd become. But … we were too late."

Amelia frowned, wrapping her hands around the warm mug as a chill swept through her. "What do you mean?"

"Annette … She made terrible choices. She let bad people into her home, let them do terrible things to her …

and to her children." Something hard settled into his eyes, though his hands remained perfectly still atop the table. "Things she managed to hide from me, until the day he was taken away."

This was the Charlie Stone Amelia knew. The cold, unforgiving man her father bought drugs from, worked for on occasion when he owed too much money. Whatever happened in the past, it was enough to bring out the killer in the old man.

"I don't understand," she said again when he fell silent. "What does that have to do with this makeshift town? This Silver City, as he calls it?"

"To understand his town, you must understand Tommy," Charles replied simply. A long moment passed, his own years of painful memories and her misperceived ones creating a gaping barrier between them. "The life Tommy knew as a child was a nightmare. Even when he awoke from that nightmare, he couldn't escape the fear. So, he created the world *he* wanted to live in, a world where he was strong enough to fight back. All the people he ever met, they all were given a place in his story, a story he created as a way to process what happened to him. Of course, this is what the doctor told us. I preferred to believe he was simply an over-imaginative boy, not wanting my own blood to display such mental incapacities, but as he grew older, we could not deny the truth any longer."

She heard the words, understood them in a sense, but didn't want to accept them. This town, this world, was not the Tommy she knew. "But, I've known Tommy since I was little. We lived on the same street until he went to live with you. But even after that, after what happened, he's always been tough. Leather jacket, cool car, fights at school. I mean, I know what happened when he was little and all, but after … He seemed totally, I don't know, normal."

"In many ways, he was. Is," Charles corrected himself. "He is not aware of what he became after that day."

As his mind took him back to that night when the truth about his daughter's addictions was revealed, Charles narrated the events to Amelia, never letting his voice waver despite the horror of what they'd found.

An otherwise quiet night had turned ominous under the threat of a debt unpaid. It had been a routine delivery, one Charlie never condoned but allowed so long as it was never discussed around him—his daughter's addiction wasn't something he could help, but he could at least make sure he knew what drugs she was poisoning her body with. None of that second-rate shit his competitors tried to pass off as the real deal.

Joe always made the deliveries. Insisted on being the one, to make sure it was done right, he claimed. Except, on this night, someone else took it upon himself to make the trip out to Iron Creek Estates. At some point neighbors had called the police with complaints of shouting and glass breaking. But such complaints were commonplace for that neighborhood, and enforcement took its time appearing at the scene.

When the officers did finally arrive, it was to discover a woman unconscious on the couch, a bruised boy huddled in a closet, and the body of a little girl wrapped in his arms, yellow hair soaked in dried blood.

"They say the bond between twins can never be broken," Charles finished, staring down at the untouched mug between his palms. "When Finley died, some part of

Tommy died with her and created a hole he could only fill with this."

One hand lifted, gesturing to the city before them. "After that night, Tommy ceased to exist. He became someone else. He portrayed himself as he lives in his Silver City, a tough child untouched by his surroundings, but every day he came home, and added to this place. New people he met, new situations that happened. He recreated it all here, putting his life into this other, make-believe world. Sometimes I think the only place life was ever real for him, was here."

Letting out a breath, Amelia took a moment to let his words sink in. She too remembered that day clearly. Finley had been her friend, so happy and perky and with big dreams of being a princess despite the poverty that surrounded her. But then she had died, beaten to death by one of her mother's junkie friends, though no one ever knew why—or who had done it. Tommy had been taken away the next day.

Not wanting to dive back into the memories of that gruesome murder, Amelia focused on another part of Charles's words. "I always wondered why he never took me to his new place when he said he moved out. He said he moved to Silver City. I thought that was just his way of saying he wasn't all that into me." She laughed softly at herself. "But now I guess I realize he couldn't bring me here, not really..."

She'd been so angry with Tommy, with his refusal to let her into his life. How foolish, how blind, could she have been to not see how much he had been hurting all these years? What kind of girlfriend was she to never know? And yet...

"You said everyone he met was part of his world. So … does that mean I'm in it?"

Now his eyes did meet hers. Amelia, the black-haired girl Tommy had held on to his entire life, the only constant after everything else had been taken away. Reaching into his coat pocket, Charles retrieved the small wooden figurine he'd taken from Tommy's pocket, not wanting him to see or have it once the drugs wore off. The figure of a young woman, yellow-painted hair and vivid blue eyes, a true testament to his grandson's wood and metalworking talent. He handed it to her, the only semblance of peace and comfort he had to offer.

"Amelia … did Tommy ever tell you about his friend named Snow?"

CHAPTER 23

HOURS AFTER THE young woman with flowing black hair fled the house, muttering apologies and trying hard to hide the panic in her eyes, Charles sat at his grandson's bedside.

He'd sent everyone home, preferring to be alone with the only family he had left. No more doctors and nurses. No more medication. It was time to bring his grandson out of this, one way or another, and it would be done without any prying eyes or ears.

Already he could see Tommy slowly starting to wake. So he waited, sitting tall in the seat, mind going over twenty years' worth of mistakes. "Your mother refused help since she was a teenager," he said to no one in particular. "I gave up on her. In turn, I gave up on her children. It was a mistake."

There was no time for grandchildren in his work. No room for family meals, holidays with kids. His wife had been the heart of their relationship, him the muscle. By the time she convinced him to take a vested interest in the kids' lives, it was too late. Finley had been murdered, and Tommy was lost to his own mind.

"All this time, I never knew it was my own right hand that killed my granddaughter. Your mother always said she didn't know who, that he wore a mask. But you knew." Charles thought back to all the conversations with Annette. How adamantly she insisted she didn't remember who was there that night, where she got the drugs, who left her children battered and bruised in the bedroom closet. He remembered so clearly their investigations, only now seeing how foolish he had been.

"All this time," he said again with a shake of his head, "thinking the mysterious killer got away, because that's exactly what Joe wanted me to believe. But you knew. Somehow, you knew. Just like you knew if Joe went with you, he'd bring DU out of hiding."

For years, Charles had looked at his grandson like an invalid. A disturbed child trapped in a young man's body. He entertained the boy's wild notions of being some kind of crime-lord kingpin, giving him slum runs and basic duties, never assigning any real responsibilities, never believing him capable. And all along Finn had been living with the faces of those who hurt him, hurt his sister.

"*A manifestation of grief and trauma,*" Dr. Jenn had explained Snow's existence once. "*He is so young and has been through something so awful, that this little girl, Snow, is the only way he can process the world. He can't process losing Finley, let alone the way she died. Snow keeps her alive. From what little he's told me about her, he's given this Snow a wonderful life.*"

"A life you both never had," Charles considered, wondering if Snow's abduction had been real in Tommy's mind or if it had all been an elaborate plot to seek revenge—or maybe even both. "Brilliance in insanity," he murmured. It pained him to know his wife's passing had been the spark to Finn's fall into that insanity, but it also gave him some amount of comfort to finally have his granddaughter avenged.

Movement on the bed pulled Charles from his thoughts. He watched as Tommy began to stir, so peaceful compared to his earlier fits, and blue eyes so closely matching his own opened. "Good morning," Charles greeted, trying hard to keep his tone warm and soothing.

Instead of answering, Tommy blinked a few times before pushing himself up to a sitting position. His movements were sluggish, as were his thoughts. "Charlie? What's going on?"

"Do you know who I am?"

"What?" Tommy grimaced, lifting a hand to his head and wondering why the hell it hurt so badly. "What do you mean? You're Charlie, my boss."

Mouth set in a curious frown, the older man pressed his fingertips together thoughtfully. "Do you want to know how Tommy's doing?"

"Tommy? Who the hell is Tommy?"

Who indeed, Charlie thought. Tommy the seven-year-old little brother was the one piece of the puzzle he couldn't figure out. The little brother who apparently no longer existed. "Do you have a brother?"

The look Tommy gave him was nothing short of exasperation. "I don't have any siblings. You know that. What the fuck are you talking about?"

"Nothing," Charlie answered softly, though he doubted the replay was heard. Tommy was still grabbing his head. "Your mother..."

The words died on his tongue the longer he watched the boy go through some sort of internal struggle. It wasn't the time to speak of Annette's death. Nor was it the time to rehash the past week. Tommy didn't seem to hear the attempt.

"Why is it so quiet?" he asked. One finger tapped his temple hard. "I don't hear anything."

"You hear me."

"I don't hear her," Tommy insisted, sitting up farther in bed and feeling his thoughts clear as more of the sedative wore off. His eyes started to turn wild though he held on to control as he stared over at his boss. "Joe and DU ... Did they..."

He knew the answer by the way Charlie looked away. Breathing suddenly became impossible. "But ... I tried, Charlie. Joe ... How did he..."

"He drugged you." That much Charlie knew to be true based on blood tests he'd had ordered. "I don't know why. I can only assume he thought you were plotting against him. He brought you to a motel just past the Georgia line, where DU came for a visit."

"He left me there," Tommy affirmed. "He didn't think I would be the one to make it out."

A week ago, Charlie wouldn't have bet on his grandson either.

"DU," Tommy continued as the attack came back to him. The fight, the piece of metal jabbing into DU's neck, the blood. So much of it, everywhere. "Shit, Charlie. I ... I killed him. What if the cops—"

"It's taken care of," Charlie cut in, giving Tommy a pointed look. "We tracked you to Georgia, to the motel where Joe brought you, then to Iron Creek." At Tommy's questioning look, he added, "Did you really think I let any of my employees drive around without me keeping tabs on them?"

Tommy didn't reply. Instead he looked down at his hands—killing hands, hands that had taken a life without second thought. And, oddly, he felt no regret. Not after all the things DU had done to him as a little boy. Collection for a debt his mother couldn't pay, he always said. He only wished he could have also put the bullet in Joe's head. Vengeance for what he did to Snow.

"They were bad people." At the affirmation, Tommy looked over at Charlie, whose expression was steady. "I only wish I'd known sooner just how bad they were. I would have tracked DU down myself and slit him open. And Joe ... Well, things would have been very different."

"I tried to get back," Tommy muttered, pressing the heels of his hands against his eyes. "I tried to beat him back. I failed, and now it's so quiet. I can't hear her anymore. She's gone."

Charlie couldn't stand the look of such heartache on the boy's face. "She's not gone, son." When Finn's hands dropped, Charlie offered a single nod. "She's still with you. You just have to find her again."

Charlie decided then that he'd put together enough pieces of the puzzle. Whoever Tommy was, an imaginary little brother, a figment of the past, he was gone in the wake of Joe and DU's deaths. Whatever Snow was to Finn, a tool for revenge, a memory of his deceased sister, or even a genuine friend, she was the existence his mind had chosen.

He couldn't force his grandson out of the made-up world. All he could do was protect him, and let him find his happiness wherever possible.

CHAPTER 24

"HELLO, AMELIA. COME in."

Amelia offered a small smile, taking a moment to observe him as she passed by. He'd become so much older in the few days since she'd last seen him, a recent widower grieving for his departed wife while also caring for his grandson, and yet also trying to maintain his usual air of superiority.

"I'm sorry I didn't come back sooner. I … I needed time to process."

"No need to apologize." Charlie stepped aside to let the young woman in. As she passed, he gave her a quick onceover. Shadows colored her eyes and her hair was unbrushed, normally stylish clothes replaced with a simple pair of jeans and black tank top.

This was a young woman aching for the man she loved. A man who would likely never come back to her.

He couldn't let her see Finn without preparation. It

wouldn't be good for either one of them. "I should warn you, Amelia. It's been a long week, and … Tommy is not doing well."

"What do you mean?"

"Come." Without further explanation, he led her to the kitchen, to a window overlooking the backyard. From the vantage point they could see deep into the yard and into one small corner of Silver City.

And there, through the window, Amelia watched Finn. From a distance, he looked like the same man she'd known for almost twenty years, that worn leather jacket covering broad shoulders, tousled blonde hair always seeming to fall in just the right place, a strikingly hand-some face shadowed by a haunting secret—a secret she now knew.

Even from here she could see the tense set of his shoulders, the stress set in his jaw, the anxiety in each step. This was not the carefree man she'd come to know and love. He was tormented, and she needed to be there to comfort him. Unable to help herself, Amelia left the kitch-en and slipped outside, determined to help him through whatever ailed his heart.

Lost in his own quiet mutterings, Finn didn't notice her approach. She tread carefully upon the dew-dropped grass, stopping when she reached the entrance to the hid-den village and leaning against the stone wall, ears trained on the quiet words floating on chilly air.

"Where are you?" he was whispering, kneeling along the main road of Silver City, fingers touching the heads of each figure in a garden surrounded by wildflowers. Not finding what, or who, he was looking for, he moved on, to a small building vaguely resembling a school. "I can't hear you. Where are you? Where did you go?"

Her heart ached as she watched the broken boy before her, so lost in his fabricated world, so desperately needing it to be real. Whatever happened in the past week—Charlie wouldn't tell her everything, only enough for her to know he'd found the people responsible for his sister's death after his grandmother's passing—it had overwhelmed him. Taken from him what was left of his reality, sending him deeper into an imagination crafted by tragedy.

A tear slipped down her cheek. Then another, each one a separate realization of the illusion she was only just now recognizing as one. She cried for Finn, a man so strong he held in twenty years of anguish until finally reaching his breaking point. She cried for the relationship they would never have again, one built upon a fictional life leading to an impossible future. And she cried for Finley, the little girl she played with as a child, always teasing her friend over her love of princesses and snowmen.

Recognition dawned on her, bringing Amelia's eyes to the plastic tiara placed among the mountain range along the outskirts of Silver City. She'd been so caught up in the beauty of the town before she hadn't taken the time to re-member where she'd seen the crown before.

"No princess is complete without her tiara," Amelia's mother had said as she placed the gift on top of Finley's head. It had been her seventh birthday, only a month be-fore her death, and the twins had been invited to Amelia's house for dinner. Their own mother hadn't even remem-bered, let alone planned anything special.

"So lame. Princesses are so *girly,"* Amelia had teased from the dinner table, her good-natured chide earning her a stern look from her mother. But Finley hadn't been upset.

No, she loved her princesses and dreams of marrying Prince Charming, and eventually convinced them all to bundle up in thick winter coats in order to build snowmen in the front yard.

Amelia smiled as she recalled the pathetic little snowman they made, barely two feet high with four lumpy sections to make a body, tiny stick arms, button eyes, and a pink cape that had once been Amelia's baby blanket.

"*She needs something,*" Finley had declared, one skinny finger to her lips as she considered what was missing. Then she smiled, her entire face lighting up, and took the tiara from her head, gently setting it on top of the snowman and making sure it was centered. "*Now she's a princess. Princess Snow.*"

"*You're such a nerd,*" her brother put in, though he too was grinning.

In response, Finley had launched a snowball at his head, and so began an hour filled with childish squeals, a girl so excited to celebrate a friend's birthday, and siblings who completed one another in every way possible.

Princess Snow. A three-dollar tiara. A birthday in the middle of winter. Memories from so long ago now coming back right before her eyes.

How could things so seemingly insignificant hold such power?

Amelia let out an incredulous breath, wiping the tears from her cheeks. She needed to be strong and help Finn through troubled times. "Tommy," she called softly from the stone entrance, not wanting to startle him out of his mutterings. He didn't answer, didn't respond at all. Closing her eyes, she searched for the strength to try again, but to try in a way that meant giving in to the fantasy.

"F-Finn?"

Now he jumped, spinning on his heel and staring at her as though startled someone else knew where his city existed. Those seductive blue eyes focused on her so intently she nearly took a step back. He saw through her, through time and reality itself, his mind connecting pieces she couldn't see but could feel in the weight of his stare.

"Amelia," he breathed, the single word containing all the hurt in his heart and soul. He approached her slowly, pulling her into a tight embrace, strong arms holding her so close as though he feared she would slip away. It felt good to be in his arms, comfortable and familiar. For a moment he simply held her, head buried against her shoulder, before he whispered, "I'm sorry. I'm so sorry."

Frowning, Amelia asked, her voice muffled against his jacket, "For what?"

"I failed her. I couldn't save her. I'm so sorry."

Amelia pulled back enough to look him in the eyes, those tormented, ice-blue eyes. "Failed who?"

Now he released her, not able to meet her confused gaze again. "Your little sister. Snow. I failed her. I tried so hard to bring her home to you. I just…"

When he trailed off, turning back to Silver City and continuing his search for objects unknown, Amelia asked, "You just what?"

"It's so quiet," he answered, dropping to his knees in an area she assumed was a forest. Trees were crushed beneath his weight, but he didn't notice as his hands went to his head. "It's too quiet. Snow's voice … She was always here with me. Now she's gone. It's so quiet. I can't … It's too quiet. Nothing makes sense."

With that, Amelia agreed. It didn't make sense. Silver

City, Finley's murder, this imaginary girl who apparently was also her little sister. She wanted her old life back, where she no longer mourned her friend's death and loved a man who was as charming as he was tough. There was no going back to that life now. All she could do was help him find his way back to his own.

"It ... it wasn't your fault. It's okay ... Finn." She had to get him out of his city, away from a fake world filled with fake people, give him a return to real life. Taking his arm, she attempted to gently steer him away. "We'll survive this somehow. We have to accept it and move on. It's ... it's what she would want."

"No." He shook his head and yanked his arm out of her grasp. "I won't accept it. Charlie said she wasn't gone. We just have to find her." Again his hands pressed over his ears, closing out the world around him. "We have to listen. If I can hear her again, we can find her. I have to hear her."

The anguished words pricked at her heart and she wanted desperately to take his hands from his head, stop them from tugging at his hair, but knew her efforts would be in vain. He was suffering the worst kind of hurt—the knowledge that after all his hoping, praying, dreaming, *trying*, after giving Snow a brand-new perfect life, he still couldn't save the girl who held his heart. There were no words to make this better. No medicines, no doctors.

She had but one offering to give the hurting boy.

With a hard swallow and desolate sigh, Amelia resigned herself to what she had to do. She reached into her pocket while stepping over the cobblestone road to where he was crouched by the miniature cemetery. Kneeling at his side, one arm around his shoulder, Amelia held her hand out in front of her. Caught in his grief, he didn't notice.

"Finn," she whispered, waiting until he looked at her, then followed her eyes down to her hand.

His breath left him, the sound a mix of shock, disbelief, and joy. With trembling fingers, Finn took the figure from her palm, cradling it in his own. "Snow. But..." He looked up at Amelia with a small shake of his head. "Charlie said she—"

"Charlie was wrong."

Gingerly, as though holding a newborn child, Finn straightened, then picked his way across Silver City to a small smattering of houses. His footsteps were meticulously placed. Amelia saw the deliberate footings that allowed him to travel his city without destroying his creations, paths made to blend in with each street and hill of the natural land.

Finn moved to the largest house in a white-picket neighborhood. It was a cozy home with white walls, a long driveway, and a wide backyard decorated in an array of tiny tables and chairs perfect for large family and friend gatherings. By one of those tables sat two paperclip parents side by side, across from them a wooden black-haired girl, the fourth chair empty.

A smile broke out on Finn's tired face as he placed the figure in that empty chair. His hand lingered on the girl's head, fingers trembling in the aftershock of finally getting her back.

"You're home, Snow," he whispered in a tone so relieved it brought fresh tears to Amelia's eyes. "Just like I promised."

There was a shift in him then, one even Amelia could

see, and she knew without him saying a word that his world was no longer a quiet one.

She lost all sense of time as she watched him, only her eyes tracing his path through the town as he moved people and vehicles around, building entire days in just minutes. A party at a house along the outskirts of town, a black Mustang speeding along the street, an ambulance bringing a woman to the hospital, a showdown at the bright-green trailer. And then, a reunion with the golden-haired girl and her family, a wood-carved boy with matching blue eyes joining them for a meal. Occasionally his lips would move as he mumbled to himself, other times he was completely silent while listening to a voice inside his head only he could hear.

Snow had returned to Finn.

It comforted Amelia to know he had found his peace. Even though to her it seemed he was simply playing with toys, beautiful and unique but toys nonetheless, it was clear what world he wanted, needed, to live in. And who was she to rip him out of it?

Forcing herself to look away, Amelia retreated out of Silver City, her eyes welling with unshed tears, cheeks stained with those already fallen. Finn didn't detect her exit, consumed with a conversation in his mind as he moved people around his city of a restructured earth. Only when she reached the patio did she realize Charles was still watching from the kitchen window. He gave her a small nod before turning away, leaving Finn to his world, telling her to do the same.

"Finntastic." Behind her, Finn chuckled, shaking his head to himself, the wide grin on his face purer than she'd ever seen before. "Only you, Snow."

With a final look back, Amelia let Finn's deep voice fill her one last time. She couldn't help but smile at how happy he was, no longer tormented, no longer at war with the silence. Part of her wondered if he'd ever come back to her, in any way. Another part acknowledged that Tommy was gone, and had been since the day his sister left him alone.

"Take care of him, Snow," Amelia whispered, tear-coated brown eyes lifting to the sky for only a moment as she remembered her friends as they used to be, who they could have been. She didn't need to understand. She only needed to accept.

And so she said her silent good-bye, leaving the boy named Finn to the story he'd created, taking with her the chaos of her own cruel world.

ACKNOWLEDGEMENTS

2015 HAS BEEN a trying year, writing often taking a backseat to focus on important home and personal matters. But, through it all, I have had an amazing network of friends, family, and colleagues there to be my shoulders to lean against. *The Silent Sounds of Chaos* was a labor of love, and many people were part of the journey.

First and foremost, thank you to my husband for never giving up on me, putting up with my long hours at the computer, and indulging me in my Dorito addiction. But, also, for not being afraid to challenge me, particularly with *The Silent Sounds of Chaos*. Your first words upon hearing the original ending to the book were, "Then what the hell is the point of even writing the book?"—and that reaction and subsequent discussion inspired me to rework the novel into something far more meaningful.

For my family, who has shown so much love and support in all aspects of my life this year. I am blessed with amazing parents, grandparents, brother, aunts, uncles, everyone, who will drop everything if it means being there for one another. Thank you for all the help, pep talks, and inspiration.

For Renee Fountain and Gandolfo Helin and Fountain Literary Management, thank you for taking a chance on a relatively unknown author and believing in me for my writing. I have loved working with you and look forward to everything we can accomplish together.

For my Thunderdome girls—you know who you are. You have no idea how much it means to have your support, and a place to talk about all the ups and downs of life. Y'all are the best! And a special shoutout to Go for giving me Duane/DU's name.

For my beta readers—Heather Lyons, Kristi Strong, Mary Hutchings, Emily Cyr, and Cindy, my momma. You guys are awesome! Thank you for your honest feedback and your excitement in reading the early draft of *The Silent Sounds of Chaos*. I loved having you part of the writing process.

For my brilliant editor, Juli Valenti. Thank you for not only being an amazing editor, but also a good friend whose unwavering excitement and support inspire me every day. I'm so happy our paths crossed in Orlando.

And, finally, for my readers—thank you for continuing to read and support my novels. I always hope to entertain with each and every book, and I sincerely hope *The Silent Sounds of Chaos* does not disappoint!

ABOUT THE AUTHOR

KRISTINA CIRCELLI IS the author of several fiction novels, including *The Helping Hands* series and *The Whisper Legacy*.

Her latest series, *The Whisper Legacy*, features *Beyond the Western Sun*. This book is what all fantasy adventures must strive to be: a complex, intricate examination of human emotion set within the context of worlds known only in our imagination. Melding fantasy and legend in an epic quest, this series signals the arrival of Kristina Circelli as a master storyteller and an important voice in Native American literature.

A descendent of the Cherokee nation and niece of a Cherokee elder, Circelli holds both a Bachelor of Arts and Master of Arts in English from the University of North Florida, where she also teaches creative writing.

To find out more about Kristina and her books visit:

Website
http://www.kristinacircelli.com/

Blog
http://anawfullybigadventure-kc.blogspot.com/

Facebook
https://www.facebook.com/AuthorKristinaCircelli/

Twitter
https://twitter.com/KCircelli

OTHER BOOKS BY KRISTINA CIRCELLI

The Whisper Legacy:

Beyond the Western Sun
Walk the Red Road
Into the Shadow Realm

The Helping Hands Series:

The Helping Hands
Shadows in the Night
The Iron Fist: Legacy of the Helping Hands
Abandon

Standalone Novels:

The Sour Orange Derby
The Never
Fade into the Woodwork
A Single Swim
Damsel Not

Short Stories:

Dungeon